JIM THE BOY

Also by Tony Earley

Here We Are In Paradise

JIM THE BOY

A NOVEL

TONY EARLEY

LITTLE, BROWN AND COMPANY

Boston · New York · London

PORTIONS OF THIS BOOK ORIGINALLY APPEARED IN
The Oxford American, The New Yorker, Brightleaf, AND *Granta.*

LIBRARY OF CONGRESS CATALOGING-IN-PUBLICATION DATA
Earley, Tony.
    Jim the boy : a novel / Tony Earley. — 1st ed.
        p.   cm.
    ISBN 0-316-19964-8
    I. Title
PS3555.A685J55   2000
813'.54 — dc21   99-42901
    ISBN 0-316-19945-1 (pbk.)

            10   9   8   7   6   5   4   3   2   1

                        Q-FG

PRINTED IN THE UNITED STATES OF AMERICA

For
Sarah California

"I love it here in the barn," said Wilbur.
"I love everything about this place."

— E. B. WHITE
Charlotte's Web

CONTENTS

Book III: Town Boys and Mountain Boys

Book IV: Cold Nights

Book V: Quiet Days

Book VI: The View from Up Here

ACKNOWLEDGMENTS

The author would like to thank the following people and institutions, whose support, moral and otherwise, made writing this book possible: Gordon Kato, Charles and Reba Earley, Donald and Ruth Bell, Trinity Episcopal School for Ministry, the Seaside Institute, the University of the South, and Vanderbilt University.

The title *Jim the Boy* was appropriated from a book of that name, published by Jim Washburn of Lake Lure, North Carolina, in 1952. The author would like Mr. Washburn's family to know that he would not have used Mr. Washburn's title if he had been able to think of a better one of his own.

Prologue

Mr. Amos Glass
Lynn's Mountain, N.C.

June 16, 1924

Dear Mr. Glass,

It is with a heavy heart that I write to you today, for your son Jim Glass, age twenty-three, has gone to live with the Lord. Just over a week ago, Jim went off alone to hoe cotton in the morning and did not return to the house at noon. My brother Al found him in the field where he had fallen, already dead. The doctor said that his heart had failed him and that he had not suffered long. I understand that Jim's mother died in a similar manner at a young age, and it is a sad, sad thing that one man should have to hear such news delivered twice in one lifetime, and I am deeply sorry for you today.

As you know, Jim was married to my sister Elizabeth, whom we know as Cissy. Cissy has taken Jim's death particularly hard and is not well. Because you and Jim have been estranged with each other these last several years, she asked me to refrain from writing you until after Jim was buried, and I have honored her request, as she was his wife. Also in accordance with her wishes, we provided Jim with Christian burial in the field where he fell, and have ordered a suitable stone to mark his final resting place and a fence to enclose it from the world. I am sorry that you did not have the opportunity to make right with Jim the things that came between you, for even though I came to love Jim as my brother and thank God for the precious time that he lived as a member of my family, the times I remember most these sad days are the occasions when I could have spoken to him with more patience and kindness than I did. I pray that as he lay dying he bore me no ill will in his heart.

But enough sadness!

I also write to you today with news of the happiest sort. Yesterday Cissy gave birth to a son, your grandson, whom she named Jim Glass in memory of his father. Jim is a fine, heavy boy with yellow hair and good lungs. Though there is still much sadness in our house, Jim's arrival in this world has reminded us that life goes on and it is God's will that we continue to do His work, even when we are sad and do not understand His plan. Each time Jim cries it is a call to arms for all of us here to do our best, as well as a reminder of our Savior's love. (How much greater our grief if Jim was not here!) As I mentioned earlier, Cissy is not well and is in no condition to receive visitors at this time. It is my hope that at some point in the future the time will be right for you to meet your grandson and have him lift the grief off of you as he has begun to do for us.

Mr. Glass, it is my solemn promise to you that we will raise Jim in the heart of our family and see with God's help that he becomes the kind of man his father would have wanted him to be. Jim was a good, Christian man and a hard worker and part of us, as he was part of you, and his name will not be forgotten as long as his son walks this earth in his footsteps.

I hope this letter finds you well and that the joy it contains eases the sadness you must at this time feel and I can't even imagine.

I am,

Yours sincerely,
Zeno McBride (Jim's brother-in-law)

BOOK I

Birthday Boy

Breakfast

DURING THE night something like a miracle happened: Jim's age grew an extra digit. He was nine years old when he went to sleep, but ten years old when he woke up. The extra number had weight, like a muscle, and Jim hefted it like a prize. The uncles' ages each contained two numbers, and now Jim's age contained two numbers as well. He smiled and stretched and sniffed the morning. Wood smoke; biscuits baking; the cool, rivery smell of dew. Something not quite daylight looked in his window, and something not quite darkness stared back out. A tired cricket sang itself to sleep. The cricket had worked all night. Jim rose to meet the waiting day.

Jim's mother opened the stove door with a dishrag. Mama was tall and pale and handsome; her neck was long and white. Although she was not yet thirty years old, she wore a long, black skirt that had belonged to her mother. The skirt did not make her seem older, but rather made the people in the room around her feel odd, as if they had wandered into an old photograph, and did not know how to behave. On the days Mama wore her mother's long clothes, Jim didn't let the screen door slam.

"There he is," Mama said. "The birthday boy."

Jim's heart rose up briefly, like a scrap of paper on a breath of wind, and then quickly settled back to the ground. His love for his mother was tethered by a sympathy Jim felt knotted in the dark of his stomach. The death of Jim's father had broken something inside her that had not healed. She pulled the heaviness that had once been grief behind her like a plow. The uncles, the women of the church, the people of the town, had long since given up on trying to talk her into leaving the plow where it lay. Instead they grew used to stepping over, or walking inside, the deep furrows she left in her wake. Jim knew only that his mother was sad, and that he figured somehow in her sadness. When she leaned over to kiss him, the lilaced smell of her cheek was as sweet and sad at once as the smell of freshly turned earth in the churchyard.

"Oh, Jimmy," she said. "How in the world did you get to be ten years old?"

"I don't know, Mama," Jim said, which was the truth. He was as amazed by the fact as she was. He had been alive for ten years; his father, who had also been named Jim Glass, had been dead for ten years and a week. It was a lot to think about before breakfast.

Mama put the biscuits she pulled from the oven into a straw basket. Jim carried the basket into the dining room. The uncles sat around the long table.

"Who's that?" Uncle Coran said.

"I don't know," said Uncle Al.

"He sure is funny-looking, whoever he is," said Uncle Zeno.

"Y'all know who I am," said Jim.

"Can't say that we do," said Uncle Coran.

"I'm Jim."

"Howdy," said Uncle Al.

"Y'all stop it," Jim said.

The uncles were tall, skinny men with broad shoulders and big hands. Every morning they ate between them two dozen biscuits and a dozen scrambled eggs and a platter of ham. They washed it all down with a pot of black coffee and tall glasses of fresh milk.

"Those biscuits you got there, Jim?" said Uncle Zeno.

Jim nodded.

"Better sit down, then."

In all things Jim strove to be like the uncles. He ate biscuits and eggs until he thought he was going to be sick. When Uncle Zeno finally said, "You think you got enough to eat, Doc?" Jim dropped his fork as if he had received a pardon.

Uncle Zeno was Jim's oldest uncle. His age was considerable, up in the forties somewhere. Uncle Coran and Uncle Al were twins. Each of them swore that he did not look like the other one, which of course wasn't true. They looked exactly alike, until you knew them, and sometimes even then. Not one of the uncles found it funny that they lived in identical houses. Uncle Al and Uncle Coran built their houses when they were young men, but, like Uncle Zeno, they never took wives. Most of the rooms in their houses didn't even have furniture; only Uncle Zeno's house had a cookstove.

Jim's mother cooked and cleaned for the uncles. When she said it was too much, the uncles hired a woman to help her. Uncle Coran ran the feed store and cotton gin. Uncle Al managed the farms. Uncle Zeno farmed with Uncle Al and operated the gristmill on Saturday mornings. As the head of the family he kept an eye on everyone else. Occasionally the uncles grew cross with each other, and, for a few days, Uncle Al and Uncle Coran would retire to their houses immediately after supper. There they sat by their own fires, or on their own porches, and kept their own counsel until their anger passed. In general, however, everyone in the family got along well with everyone else; to Jim, the sound of harsh words would always strike his ear as oddly as a hymn played in the wrong key.

Jim patted his stomach. "That ought to hold me till dinner," he said.

"You ate a right smart," Uncle Coran said.

"Well," said Jim, "I am ten years old now."

"My, my," said Uncle Al.

"I've been thinking it's about time for me to go to work with y'all," Jim said.

"Hmm," said Uncle Zeno.

"I thought maybe you could use some help hoeing that corn."

"We can usually put a good hand to work," Uncle Zeno said. "You a good hand?"

"Yes, sir," said Jim.

"You ain't afraid to work?"

"No, sir."

"What do you say, boys?" Uncle Zeno said.

Uncle Al and Uncle Coran looked at each other. Uncle Coran winked.

"He'll do, I guess," said Uncle Al.

"Let's get at it, then," said Uncle Zeno.

A Day of Work

AFTER BREAKFAST Uncle Coran went off to open the store. Jim rode to the field in the truck with Uncle Zeno and Uncle Al. He stood on the bed of the truck and looked out over the top of the cab. He held on to his straw hat with one hand and the truck with the other. The world at that early hour seemed newly made, unfinished; the air, still sweet with dew, an invention thought up that morning. In the low places near the river, stray ghosts of fog still hunted among the trees. The state highway led directly into the rising sun; when the sun pulled itself loose from the road, it suddenly seemed very far away. The sky, in a moment Jim didn't notice until the moment had passed, turned blue, as if it had never tried the color before and wasn't sure anyone would like it. Jim giggled out loud for no reason he could think of.

Five field hands met them at the edge of the river bottom. The field hands were black men who lived in the woods on the hill behind the new school. They walked over without saying much and took hoes out of the bed of the truck. Jim grabbed the newest hoe for himself. Its handle was still shiny and smooth with varnish, its blade not yet darkened by rust. Uncle Zeno shook his head.

"Give that one to Abraham, Doc," he said.

Abraham had white hair. He could remember the day a soldier told him he was free. He was the father or grandfather of most of the people who lived on the hill. Jim did not want to give Abraham his hoe.

"I want to use this one," Jim said.

"I'll use this one here," Abraham said. He took the last hoe from the truck bed. Its handle was broken off about halfway down. All the other hoes had been taken already.

"That one's for Jim," Uncle Zeno said. He took the new hoe from Jim's hands. Abraham handed Jim the hoe with the broken handle. Jim knew better than to say anything else.

"Let's get some hoeing done," said Uncle Zeno.

"By dinnertime you'll be glad you've got that hoe," Abraham said. "It's nice and light."

Jim was still angry. "I'm ten years old today," he said.

"My, my," said Abraham.

Jim walked with the uncles and the field hands through the wet grass to the far end of the bottom. The grass soaked the legs of his overalls; the cloth was cold against his skin. The men fell out of line one by one and arranged themselves two rows apart. Each man would hoe to the end of one row and then back up the other. Then they would walk to the end of the line and take up two more rows. In this way they would hoe the whole field. Jim took up the two rows beside Uncle Zeno.

The corn was knee-high to the uncles, but almost waist-high to Jim. The field contained thirty acres. It would take several days to hoe it all. Then, after the hoeing was completed, Uncle Al would come back with the mules and the cultivator, and plow the middles of the rows. The field would then be free of grass and weeds; the corn could grow without competition. At the end of the summer there would be more to sell and grind into meal and feed to the mules.

Uncle Zeno stepped into Jim's corn row. Jim's cheeks flushed. He could feel the field hands watching him.

"You do it like this, Doc," Uncle Zeno said. "You put the blade of the hoe against the stalk and then pull it toward you. That way you don't hack the corn down."

"I know how to hoe," Jim said.

"Show me," said Uncle Zeno.

Jim chopped at a small clump of grass. The hoe blade bit cleanly into a cornstalk. The cornstalk fell slowly over, like a tree. Jim heard a field hand laugh.

"That's one lick," Uncle Zeno said.

Uncle Zeno had never whipped Jim, but Jim was always afraid that he might. Uncle Zeno kept a running count of the licks he was saving for Jim. He said he had them written down in a book. When Jim did something good, he said he erased a lick or two. Jim figured that most of the time he ran a lick or two short of break-even.

"It's this hoe," Jim said. The end of the broken handle was as sharp as the point of a spear.

Uncle Zeno got down on one knee and looked Jim in the face. "Jim," he said. "I ain't got time to argue with you about that hoe and listen to excuses. Do you want to help me, or do you want to go home?"

"I want to help you," Jim said.

"All right, then. Watch."

Uncle Zeno dragged his hoe sharply across the clump of grass Jim had missed. The grass came up cleanly, and he scraped it into the middle of the row.

"Now you do it."

Jim scraped up a small sprig of clover. "That's good," Uncle Zeno said. "That hoe works after all."

Uncle Zeno stepped back into his own row. The field hands and Uncle Al were already at work. Uncle Al was slightly ahead of the line. None of the uncles liked to be beaten at anything. Jim didn't like to lose, either. He decided he would beat Abraham to the far end of the field. Then after dinner Uncle Zeno would give the broken hoe to Abraham. Maybe Uncle Zeno would tell Abraham to go home.

Without looking up, Jim carefully scraped the ground clean around the first ten stalks of corn in his row. He piled the weeds and grass up in neat piles. At the tenth stalk, he ran into a clump of grass that was too tough to dig up with his hoe. He got down on his knees and pulled at it with both hands. It wouldn't budge. He stuck the sharp point of his hoe handle underneath the grass and pried at it. He pulled and pried at the grass until the roots finally came loose with a ripping noise. Jim hoisted the clump of grass into the air like a trophy, or a large fish. Its roots held a clod of dirt as big as a cat. He looked around to see if anyone saw him, but everyone was gone. He couldn't see anyone at all until he stood up. The uncles and the field hands were a hundred yards or more ahead of him, and moving away at a slow walk. Uncle Al was out in front of everyone else. Uncle Zeno and Abraham looked to be tied for second.

Jim turned and stared back at the head of his row. He could spit that far. He looked in the other direction at the end of the row in the distance. The woods along the river seemed as far away as the moon. The uncles, as far ahead of Jim as they were, had hoed less than a fourth of the way to the end of the field. Jim didn't see how he could ever make it to the end of his row, much less hoe the one beside it. He had started a journey he knew he could not finish. He felt a sob gather up in his stomach like a cloud.

That Jim felt like crying made him angry. He attacked the ground with his hoe as if he were killing snakes. He struck almost blindly at the morning glories and grass and clover, but in his fury chopped down another stalk of corn. The sob that had been waiting in his stomach climbed up out of his throat and hung in the air for a second, a small, inconsequential sound, heard only by him.

The uncles and the field hands were still moving away, hoeing as they walked. Jim was afraid he would get into trouble if Uncle Zeno found out he had chopped down another stalk of corn. He could not bear the thought of Uncle Zeno being mad at him. He got down on his knees and dug a small hole with his hands. He stuck the end of the stalk in the hole and filled the hole around it with dirt. Then he patted the dirt around the stalk so that it stood up straight.

Jim picked up his hoe and wiped his nose on the back of his arm. He wiped the back of his arm on the leg of his overalls. He felt calmer. He decided that he would hoe until dinnertime. He couldn't think of a way to get home until then, but he knew that Uncle Zeno wouldn't make him come back to the field after dinner if he didn't want to.

Jim threw a rock toward the place he had started work. He often threw rocks as a way of gauging how far away things were. He wanted to know how far he had hoed. The rock, however, was a little flat and light, and curved off short to one side. Jim hunted around until he found a better rock. Good throwing rocks were hard to find in the rich dirt of the river bottom. He threw four or five more rocks until he was satisfied that he had hoed farther than he could throw a rock. This seemed like progress.

When Jim picked up his hoe, he noticed that it was about the length of a baseball bat. He grasped the handle right above the blade and took a couple of practice swings. He found a suitable hitting rock and tossed it up in the air and swung at it with the handle. Strike one. The hoe blade made swinging the handle awkward. Jim struck out twice before he finally hit the rock. It whizzed off to the right. Foul ball. He hit three more rocks before he got in a satisfactory lick and turned his attention again to the weeds growing in the field.

Jim saw a rock at his feet that looked like an arrowhead. He dug it up with his hoe, but found that the rock was fat and round on the bottom; it only looked like an arrowhead from the top. Jim had found only one arrowhead on his own, but the uncles often brought him the ones they found. Uncle Coran was the best at finding arrowheads. He could hardly walk through a field without picking one up. When Uncle Coran was a boy, he had even found a stone knife. He kept it in a cigar box on the mantel in his bedroom, and wouldn't give it to Jim. Jim was afraid the uncles would pick up all the arrowheads in the bottoms before he got good at finding them, but Uncle Zeno said there would always be plenty of arrowheads to find. More turned up every time the fields were plowed.

Jim studied the rock in his hand closely. Maybe it had been the start of an arrowhead. He didn't think so, but he could ask Uncle Coran about it at dinnertime. Uncle Coran knew a lot about how the Indians had lived. Uncle Coran said that Indians had started their fires by hitting two rocks together. Jim scraped together a small pile of dry grass and found another good-sized rock. He held the rocks close above the grass and hit them together until sparks flew off. The sparks, however, did not ignite the grass. Jim could not understand how Indians had been able to start fires like this. Nor did he understand how Indians made canoes out of tree bark, or got close enough to deer to shoot them with bows and arrows. Jim often wished he were an Indian, but thought that being a cowboy would be easier. He couldn't walk in the woods without making noise, and he couldn't start a fire by hitting two rocks together. Cowboys at least got to use matches and guns, but they also had to ride bucking bulls. Jim didn't know if he would ever be brave enough to ride a bull. He began to think he would never be good at anything. The end of the field again seemed farther away than the last time he had looked.

Jim could smell sweat soaking his overalls. He touched the denim covering his thigh with the palm of his hand. The cloth was hot to the touch. Jim squinted up. The sun was small and white; the sky was devoid of color, empty even of clouds and birds. Jim tried to figure out what time it was by looking at the sun. He tried without success until he could no longer see. He could not remember ever being as hot as he was right then. There was a bucket of water in the truck, but Jim knew that you weren't supposed to drink from it until you had hoed back to the head of the field. The uncles did not believe in wasting steps. The uncles and the field hands had made the turn and were hoeing back toward Jim. They were still a long way off, but Jim knew they would see him if he went to the truck. Two drops of sweat trickled out from under

Jim's hat, and he stood still to see where they went. One drop ran into his eyes, and the other trickled down his cheek. A gnat flew into his mouth. Jim spat it out. He took off his hat and waved it around his face, but could not make the gnats go away.

"What are you doing down there, Doc?" Uncle Zeno asked.

Jim jumped. He had not noticed Uncle Zeno's shadow cover the ground where he crouched. "I'm looking at this praying mantis," said Jim.

"Did it bite you?"

"No."

Jim had knocked the praying mantis off a corn stalk and chopped it in two with his hoe. He was poking at the two pieces with the sharp point of the handle.

"Praying mantises eat other bugs, Jim," Uncle Zeno said. "If you want to kill something, kill a grasshopper. Grasshoppers eat corn."

"Yes, sir," Jim said.

He covered up the two green halves of the praying mantis with dirt. He wondered if in killing it he had added another lick to Uncle Zeno's list.

"Well," said Uncle Zeno, "let's see how you've been doing." He walked back toward the head of Jim's row, looking at the ground. "You missed a lot of morning glories through here," he said, scratching at the ground as he walked. "They'll take over a field if you don't get 'em before they get up on the corn."

Uncle Zeno came to the cornstalk Jim had chopped down and stuck back in the ground. He stood and looked at it a long time. Then he pulled it up and turned around and looked at Jim. Uncle Zeno was extremely tall. Jim had never noticed before exactly how tall.

"What happened to this one here?" Uncle Zeno said.

"I don't know," Jim said.

"You don't know," said Uncle Zeno.

"No, sir," said Jim.

"You know it won't grow now."

Jim nodded.

"Then why did you stick it back in the ground?"

"I don't know," said Jim.

"You don't know."

"No."

Uncle Zeno held the corn stalk up like a scepter, as if seeing it better would help Jim answer his questions.

"Jim, this was just a mistake until you tried to hide it," he said. "But when you tried to hide it, you made it a lie."

Jim looked at the front of his overalls. He felt a tear start down his cheek. He snatched at it and hoped that Uncle Zeno hadn't seen it.

Uncle Zeno threw the cornstalk away from him as if it were a dirty thing, something to be ashamed of.

"Do you lie to me a lot, Jim?"

"No," Jim said.

"Should I worry about believing the things you tell me? I never have before, but should I start now?"

Jim shook his head. He wasn't able to say no again.

"What's the matter?" Uncle Zeno said.

"I don't feel good," said Jim.

"Are you sick?"

Jim shrugged.

"Go on home, then," Uncle Zeno said.

Jim looked down the row toward the river. He suddenly wanted to finish his work.

Uncle Zeno pointed in the direction of town. "Go on," he said. "If you're sick, you don't need to be out in the sun."

"I think I can make it till dinner," Jim said.

"No, you go on home and tell your mama you're sick."

Jim sent a small whimper out into the air between himself and Uncle Zeno, like a scout in advance of the protest that would follow.

"Go on," Uncle Zeno said.

From the edge of the road Jim turned around and looked back at the field. Uncle Zeno was hoeing the row Jim had abandoned. The field hands were spread out through the bottom. Uncle Al was still way out in front of everybody else. He was approaching the river for the second time that morning, working as if he would never stop.

An Unexpected Gift

JIM WALKED home through the fields and pastures. Along the way he did not try to flush baby rabbits from their hidden beds in the tall grass of the hay field. Nor, when he took off his shoes and waded across the branch, did he search among the stones for gold nuggets, or look beneath the larger rocks for crawdads and spring lizards. Jim particularly liked holding the small lizards in his cupped hands and watching their tiny hearts beat beneath the pale, thin skin of their undersides. And he liked the fierce, snapping claws of the crawdads. But today he simply crossed over to the town side of the creek, put on his shoes, and continued on his way. When he skirted the small clearing in the woods that held the abandoned tenant house where his mother had lived with his father, he didn't throw rocks onto the tin roof, nor sneak onto the creaky porch for a peek through the dirty windows.

In town, Jim swung wide of the uncles' houses.

An early appearance at home would worry Mama. She would make him lie down, and put her hand on his forehead to see if he had a fever. Sometimes she made him wear a jacket when it was warm outside. She had not wanted him to go to the cornfield, and relented only when the uncles promised to watch him every minute. Often the uncles had to rescue Jim from her tender care.

To Jim's relief, Aliceville, in the long hour before noon, was almost deserted. The dogs who might have barked or wagged their tails when Jim passed were asleep in the round holes they had dug in the cool dirt beneath some porch. The men and boys who might have been about at some other time of the day were off working. The women, Jim knew, were cooking dinner for the men to eat when they came in from the fields. The town squatted quietly in the sun as if tied to the ground by the web of crisscrossing power lines stretched between the houses.

The only person in sight was Pete Hunt, the railroad station agent. Pete was a small man with a big mustache. He sat on the porch of the depot reading a magazine. He did not like kids much. If a kid looked in the window of the freight office while Pete was using the telegraph, Pete pulled the shade down. Sometimes Pete let Jim search through the coal piles for fossils, but sometimes he came out of the depot and ran him off. Jim could never tell with Pete. He never noticed that Pete only ran him away from the coal pile when he was with another boy. Pete looked at Jim over the top of his magazine.

"Hey," said Jim.

Pete nodded once, but didn't say anything. He moved the magazine upward until it covered his eyes. Pete had wired the uncles' houses for electricity when Jim was a baby. Mama said Pete had almost lived with them for the month it took to do the job, yet he hardly spoke the whole time.

Jim moved slowly down Depot Street toward the store, although he didn't particularly want to see Uncle Coran, either. He did not want to have to explain himself. He stared at the ground, but with little interest in trying to follow any of the tracks left in the dirt. Today, Jim couldn't think of anything he wanted to do, a game he wanted to play, or a place he wanted to be. He felt sorry for himself because his birthday was turning out so poorly. He kicked a rock, but didn't watch to see how far it rolled.

Jim was in front of the hotel when Whitey Whiteside called his name from an open window upstairs. The hotel was a skinny, brick building where salesmen and railroad crews stayed while waiting in town to catch one train or another. Whitey Whiteside was a drummer for Governor Feeds. He took orders for the sacks of feed and seed that the uncles sold in the store. His given name was Ralph, but he said it was harder to forget a salesman named Whitey than it was to forget one named Ralph. Jim liked Whitey because Whitey carried rock candy in his coat pocket, and always gave Jim a piece. The uncles said Whitey Whiteside was honest; they would not buy feed or seed from other drummers.

"Hey," yelled Whitey Whiteside from the window. "Hey, Jim Glass."

Jim looked up at the hotel window. He smiled slightly before remembering how unhappy he was.

"Hey," Jim called back. "Hey, Whitey Whiteside."

"Where you going?" Whitey asked.

"Nowhere," said Jim.

"Hang on a minute, then," said Whitey. "I ain't going nowhere, either."

Jim waited while Whitey Whiteside clomped down the stairs of the hotel and came out into the street. He was tall and skinny like the uncles. His brown hair was going gray, which he said was a good thing, even though he was young. Gray hair on a young man, he said, coupled with the name Whitey, would make people remember him even better.

"What happened to you?" Whitey asked. "You've got dirt all over your face."

"I've been hoeing corn with the uncles," said Jim.

"That's good, Jim," Whitey said. "Hard work's good for a man. Hard work will grow hair on your chest." He studied Jim closely. "But you know," he said, "you ought to carry a bandanna in your pocket, and wipe your face off with that, instead of your hand. That way, if you run into a pretty girl on your way home, you won't have dirt all over your face."

Jim shrugged. He liked Whitey Whiteside, but didn't always know what to say to him. Whitey Whiteside talked to Jim like Jim was grown. He had even asked Jim to call him "Whitey," and not "Mr. Whiteside."

"Well," Whitey said, "I don't guess it matters."

Jim shrugged again and looked at his hands. He wiped them on the legs of his overalls and then stuck them in his pockets.

Whitey Whiteside always wore a suit and a starched white shirt. He wore big fedoras with stiff brims, felt in the winter, and blazing white straw in the summer. Jim thought Whitey Whiteside must be rich.

"I mean," said Whitey, "it's probably more important to a pretty girl that a man has a good job and works hard and looks after things, than whether or not he has a little dirt on his face. Don't you guess?"

"I don't know," Jim said.

Jim and Whitey stood in the street for a long moment without talking.

"The uncles let me off a little early today," Jim said. "It was almost dinnertime, anyway."

"I see," said Whitey.

Jim studied one of his footprints in the dirt. He could see the nail marks around the outside of the sole. Jim could feel some of the nails sticking through on the inside of his shoe. The nails didn't bother him unless he thought about them. He wiggled his toes.

Whitey took his watch out of his pocket and looked at the face as if it were unfamiliar.

"Let's see here," he said. "It's still a little bit until my train pulls in, so why don't we walk up the hill and have a look at that new school?"

Whitey covered his routes by riding trains all over North Carolina. He had even ridden the Carolina Moon, which was the newest, fastest passenger train on the Great Southeastern Railway. The Moon did not stop in Aliceville.

"Okay," Jim said. "I guess we can go look."

The new school was the biggest building in Aliceville. It was two stories high and made from red brick. The hotel was the only other brick building in town, but it was narrow and dirty and sad-looking. The new school sat on top of the hill like a fortress. You could see it from all over Aliceville. It had been under construction for as long as Jim could remember. It was supposed to open in the fall. Jim and Whitey walked up the dirt street toward the school.

"That's some building, huh, Jim?" Whitey said.

Jim didn't say anything. He was nervous about going to the new school. The old school he had attended since first grade had only two rooms. Jim knew everybody who went to school there, even the older kids. But when the new school opened, all the country schools around Aliceville would close down, and the kids who went to those schools would come to school in Aliceville. They would ride to town on buses. Even hillbilly kids from Lynn's Mountain would come to the new school. Jim had often seen hillbilly kids with their fathers at the store. They stared at Jim as if they hated him already; he didn't like them, either. Jim's grandfather lived on Lynn's Mountain. Jim had never laid eyes on him, and did not think he ever would. Mama would not permit it. Jim was a little afraid of going to school with kids who might know his grandfather, but he had not told anyone that.

Jim stopped at the edge of the school yard, but Whitey Whiteside marched up the steps and tried the wide front door. It was locked.

"Shoot," Whitey said. "I was hoping we could get inside."

Whitey walked down the steps and over to the nearest window. He was just tall enough to look in. He pushed his hat back and cupped his hands around his face and peered through the glass.

"That's the principal's office, I guess," he said. "You'll need to make sure you stay out of there, Jim. You want to see what it looks like?"

Jim shook his head. He did not want to look inside the principal's office. His old school didn't have a principal, just two teachers, and they were both nice.

Whitey walked farther down the side of the building and stopped at another window.

"This'll probably be a classroom right here," he said. He peered inside and whistled. "Boy, this is something, Jim," he said. "Come have a look."

Jim shook his head again.

"Oh, come on," Whitey said. "You're not going to get into trouble for looking in the window."

He made a low step with his hands. Jim put his foot into it and Whitey hoisted him up. Jim pressed his face against the glass. The glass was warm from the sun. He had watched the school going up, but he had not looked inside before. The first thing he noticed was that the room did not have a proper ceiling. The beams holding up the second floor were visible.

"What's that up there on the ceiling?" Whitey asked.

"It doesn't have a ceiling," Jim said.

"You know what I mean," said Whitey.

"Electric lights," Jim said.

"You got it," said Whitey.

The uncles said that electricity would come to Aliceville when the new school opened, but Jim had his doubts. The town had been wired for years, but still hadn't been connected to the power plant in New Carpenter. Jim wanted to go to a school with electric lights, but he wasn't getting his hopes up.

"And look at the size of that blackboard," Whitey said. "There'll be plenty of room to do arithmetic problems. You won't have to worry about running out of space when you do algebra."

The room was empty save for the lights and the blackboard. It did not have desks in it yet, or pictures on the walls. Jim pushed away from the window and Whitey lowered him to the ground.

"Shoot, Jim," Whitey said, "you're going to get so smart you won't be able to stand it."

"The uncles are going to teach me how to do geometry," Jim said. "They're good at geometry."

"They're smart men," Whitey said, seriously. "You do what the uncles say and you'll turn out all right. That's for sure."

Jim and Whitey turned away from the school and started back toward town. They could see almost all of Aliceville from the top of the hill. Pete Hunt stood up on the porch of the depot and stretched and looked up and down the street. Uncle Coran walked out of the cotton gin and into the store. He would lock the store soon and go to Uncle Zeno's house for dinner. Smoke was rising from the kitchen chimney. Uncle Al and Uncle Zeno would come in from the field and tell Uncle Coran and Jim's mother about the morning. Jim felt something cold, like a fog, ink out through his belly. Only his mother would believe he had gotten sick in the field. The uncles would not have much to say because they would be ashamed of Jim. The tall houses on Depot Street were the last place Jim wanted to go.

Whitey suddenly slapped Jim on the arm.

"Hey," he said, "I heard it might be somebody's birthday today. You hear anything about that?"

"I don't know," Jim said. "What did you hear?"

"I heard that a certain boy might have turned ten years old today."

"I guess it's me," Jim said, as if confessing to a crime.

"It's you?"

"Yep."

"You don't say. Ten years old. You get any presents yet?"

"Nope."

"You mean your mama and the uncles didn't get you anything for your birthday?"

Jim had not considered the possibility before. If the uncles had gotten him something, they might not give it to him now. And if his mother had a present for him, why hadn't she given it to him at breakfast?

"I guess not," Jim said. The fog in his belly climbed his backbone toward his neck.

"That's terrible," Whitey said. "To have a birthday, to turn ten years old, which is pretty old, and not get one present. Don't you think that's about the most terrible thing you ever heard?"

Jim nodded. He didn't want to cry in front of Whitey, but thought he might have to.

"Well," said Whitey, "we're going to have to do something about that. Hang on a minute."

He stopped in the middle of the street. He reached into his pants pocket and pulled out half a plug of tobacco.

"You chew?" he said.

"Nope," said Jim.

"Hmm," said Whitey. He reached into one of his coat pockets and pulled out a small pad. "You got any use for a receipt book?"

Jim shook his head.

"Didn't think so," Whitey said.

He reached into his other coat pocket and rummaged around. When he removed his hand it contained a new baseball. "How about this?" he said. "Can you use a baseball?"

Jim gasped. "That's for me?" he said.

"If you can use it," said Whitey.

"I can use it!" Jim said. "I can use it! I can use it!"

"Good," Whitey said. "I'm tired of carrying it around. It made my pocket lumpy. I got it for my granny for Christmas, but she didn't have a bat."

He handed the baseball to Jim.

"Thanks, Whitey!" Jim said.

He stared at the baseball in his hand as if it were made of gold. His baseball at home was as heavy as a cannonball. He had accidentally left it out in the rain, and was afraid to ask for another one. But this baseball was brand-new. It was shinier than Whitey's hat. He felt like he could throw it a mile.

Jim tossed the baseball up into the air. Whitey reached out and caught it before it came down. "You're sure you can use it?" he said.

"WHITEY!" Jim yelled.

"All right," Whitey said. "Just checking." He handed the baseball back to Jim, and together they started back down the hill.

Baptism

WHEN THE uncles came in at midday, Jim didn't mention the baseball Whitey Whiteside had given him because he had begun to suspect that taking it was wrong. The uncles and Jim's mother ate without talking much, until late in the meal. Nobody said anything to Jim about what had happened that morning in the field. Jim decided he would hide the baseball in the barn until Whitey Whiteside came back to town. Then he would give it back.

"Pretty good morning, wasn't it Allie?" Uncle Zeno said.

"We got a right smart done, I reckon," said Uncle Al.

Uncle Zeno stirred a slice of butter into the apple cobbler Jim's mother had made for dessert. Jim had noticed already that she hadn't baked a cake.

"Seems like you got more done out there than the rest of us," Uncle Zeno said.

"I'm not fast," Uncle Al said. "The rest of y'all are just slow."

"There was a time, you know, when I didn't think you were going to make much of a farmer."

Uncle Al turned and stared at Uncle Zeno. He was vain about how he ran the farms. Uncle Coran said that Uncle Al would walk half a mile to pull a morning glory off a fence post.

"And just when was that?" Uncle Al said.

"That time you and Coran baptized all those chicks."

"Shoot, Zee," said Uncle Al. "We weren't but four years old. Ain't you ever going to forget about that?"

"Nope," said Uncle Zeno. "I got a whipping because of it. And you were five years old. It was the summer I got baptized, and I was twelve. Seeing me get baptized is where y'all got the idea."

"We were still just little fellows," Uncle Al said. "We didn't know any better."

"It was all Allie's idea, Jim," said Uncle Coran. "He was the preacher. I was just the deacon. All I did was hand him the chicks. He's the one who stuck them in the rain barrel."

"Y'all were just little knotheads," Uncle Zeno said. "Cissy wasn't even born yet, or she'd have been out there, too, helping with the service. She was bad to follow you two around and get into whatever mischief you got into."

"They were my big brothers," Jim's mother said. "I didn't think they could do anything wrong."

Uncle Zeno snorted. "You don't know the half of

it," he said. "Anyway, Jim, we had this little game hen, and she had this big flock of chicks. There must have been twelve of them."

"Thirteen," said Uncle Al.

"Thirteen," said Uncle Zeno. "And Al here, he and Coran, they had seen me get baptized down at the river, and they thought that was really something. Seven or eight of us got baptized that summer, and Coran and Al, they were standing on the bank watching everything, and listening, and their little heads filled up with ideas.

"So one Sunday afternoon, not too long after I got baptized, Corrie and Allie turned up missing, and Mama sent me out to find them. Well, when I found them, they were in the barnyard, baptizing chicks.

"They had the chicks in a peach basket, and Coran would reach into the basket and catch one and hand it to Al. And Al, he'd stick it down in the rain barrel. Then he'd hand the chick back to Coran, and Coran would fish around in the basket for a dry one."

"We thought they needed to be saved," Uncle Coran said. "We wanted them to go to heaven."

"They went to heaven all right," said Uncle Zeno. "By the time I got over there, you had drowned them all but one. I tried blowing in their bills to save them, but Al had held them under the water too long, and they had drowned.

"Well, by then, both of you had figured out you'd done something wrong, and you started crying. You cried and begged me not to tell on you, because you knew if Mama found out you had killed her chicks, she would break off a switch and whip you good.

"Now, me, I didn't want to see the two of you get whipped, so I took the dead chicks out behind the smokehouse and dug a hole and buried them. And I made you promise not to tell.

"How we got in trouble, though, is that Daddy saw me go behind the smokehouse with the hoe. In a little bit he came in the house with the chicks. He came straight up to me, and I really hadn't been involved in the thing at all, until it was too late, and he said, 'Zeno, what do you know about these dead chicks?'

"And I told him I had found them in the rain barrel, which wasn't far off the truth. Then he said, 'Zeno, how did these chicks get in the rain barrel?' and I told him I didn't know.

"He said, 'You don't know.'

"And I said, 'I don't know.'

"So, right about then, Little Allie and Little Corrie, bless their hearts, couldn't stand it anymore, and busted out crying and told Daddy that they had baptized the chicks in the rain barrel and the chicks had drowned.

"Daddy stood and thought about it a minute and said to Coran and Al, 'Boys, I'm not going to whip you, because you're little and you didn't know any better, but you better never stick another chicken in the rain barrel.'

"And then he said to me, 'Zeno, I'm not going to whip you for burying the chicks behind the smokehouse, because you were standing up for your brothers, which is admirable. But I am going to whip you for lying to me about it.'"

"What happened?" Jim asked.

"He took me outside and gave me the worst whipping I ever got in my life," Uncle Zeno said. "And I never lied to him again."

"And we never baptized any more chickens," said Uncle Coran.

"That's the truth," said Uncle Al.

"So, all in all, Jim," Uncle Zeno said, "Allie turned out to be a pretty good farmer, when you consider how he started out."

"At least we can be thankful he didn't try to become a preacher," Uncle Coran said.

"That's for sure," said Uncle Al. "I would've had to be a Methodist to keep from drowning people."

Mama stood and began clearing the dishes from the table.

"Where was the mama hen while all this was going on?" she asked.

"We locked her in the chicken house," Uncle Coran said. "She almost flogged us. We had to get after her with a couple of sticks to get her in there."

"She spent the rest of the afternoon looking for those chicks," Uncle Al said. "She looked all over the yard."

"That's sad," said Mama.

"What happened to her?" asked Jim.

"I don't remember," Uncle Zeno said. "I guess we ate her."

After Supper

THE UNCLES rocked in their tall chairs on Uncle Zeno's porch, while Mama pushed herself in the swing. Jim sat on the top step with his chin in his hands and contemplated the end of the day. The sun was low in the sky, but its reflection still burned in the windows of the new school. Soon, long, blue shadows would slide up out of the river bottoms. Fireflies would light themselves in the tops of the trees, and cicadas would chant and tree frogs would screech. Along the fence rows whippoorwills would call and listen and call again, and from deep in the grass crickets would answer with low, sad songs. Bats would dip and wheel in the purpling sky, their strange flights marked by the whisper of wings. Twilight was the loveliest time of day in Aliceville, but Jim did not want the sun to set. He did not want his birthday to end. Nothing had gone right. He had disappointed the uncles, and didn't want to wait until his next birthday, a whole year away, to make things right.

"I'm getting a little chilly," Mama said. "I'm going inside to get a sweater."

She stood up and disappeared into the house. Jim was so lost in his thoughts that he did not notice when she reappeared beside him.

"Jim," she said. "Hey, Jim."

Jim turned and looked up. Mama was holding a chocolate cake. The top of the cake was alight with burning candles. She leaned over so he could see it. The reflection of the little flames jumped in her eyes.

"Happy birthday, Jim," she said.

Suddenly the uncles were gathered around him as well. "Look at him," Uncle Al said. "I don't think he knows what it is."

"What is it?" said Uncle Coran.

"It's Jim's birthday cake," Uncle Zeno said.

"Oh," said Uncle Coran. "I thought Cissy was on fire."

Jim counted the candles on the cake. There were ten.

"Jim," Uncle Zeno said, "did you think we had forgotten you?"

"I thought you were mad at me."

"Oh, sweetie," Mama said, "don't cry. Nobody's mad at you."

"I'm not mad at you, Doc," Uncle Zeno said. "I promise."

"Zeno, I told you not to take him to the field," Mama said.

"Hush, Cissy," Uncle Zeno said quietly.

Uncle Coran hoisted Jim by his overall straps

and pretended that he was going to throw him over the banister and out into the yard.

"You knothead," he said. "You'd know it if we were mad at you. Wouldn't he, Al?"

"We'd get a stick after him if we were mad."

Jim didn't know why he was crying, only that he couldn't stop.

"Whitey Whiteside gave me a baseball," he said.

"Well," said Uncle Zeno, "wasn't that nice of Whitey? Did you thank him?"

Jim nodded.

"Good. That's how you've been raised. You better go ahead and blow out all those candles."

Jim blew out the candles with a single breath.

"I wonder if Mr. Ralph Whiteside gives baseballs to all the little boys on his route?" Mama said.

Uncle Zeno quickly and almost imperceptibly shook his head.

"Jim?" asked Uncle Al. "Can we have some of your cake?"

"I guess so," Jim said.

"We didn't get a chocolate cake on our birthday, did we Allie?" Uncle Coran said.

"We sure didn't."

"Let's go to the dining room," said Mama.

In the middle of the dining room table Jim spotted a baseball glove and a baseball bat. He stood in the doorway and stared.

"Are those *mine?*" he asked.

"Are what yours?" Uncle Zeno said.

Jim pointed at the table. Uncle Zeno leaned into the dining room and shrugged.

"Never seen them before," said Uncle Coran. "What are they?"

"Oh, stop it," Mama said. "Sometimes I could just strangle y'all."

Uncle Zeno placed his hand on Jim's back and lightly shoved him into the dining room. Jim approached the table warily, as if he might frighten off the glove and bat if he moved too quickly.

"The bat's a genuine Louisville Slugger," Uncle Zeno said. "It's probably a little big for you, so you'll have to choke up on it till you grow into it."

The bat was indeed too heavy for Jim, and more than a few inches too long. Jim slid his hands up the handle until the bat felt light and short enough to swing; the wood was smooth and cool, varnished so brightly that Jim searched the grain for his reflection.

"It's perfect," he announced. "It's just perfect."

"Now the glove," said Uncle Zeno, "is a Rawlings. I asked the man in the store in New Carpenter what kind of glove major leaguers use, and he said Rawlings. You ought to be able to catch pretty good with a glove like that."

The glove, like the bat, was also too big, a fact that Jim did not notice then, and would not notice later. The glove's fat fingers were twined together with an intricate web of rawhide laces; the wrist strap fastened with a bright brass button. Jim covered his face with the glove and inhaled deeply. It bore the luxurious, almost forbidden smell of the uncles' harness room. Jim could sit for hours in the barn while the uncles mended or oiled harnesses; he wasn't allowed to play in the harness room alone.

Jim gazed up at his mother and the uncles as if he had a wonderful story to tell them but could not remember their language. Everyone seemed as happy as if they had received a bat and glove themselves, although Mama's eyes looked a little wet.

"They're from all of us, Jim," she said. "We love you very much."

"Speak for yourself, Cissy," Uncle Coran said. "I can take him or leave him."

"He's all right, for a knothead," said Uncle Al.

"He ain't no bigger than a poot," said Uncle Zeno, "but I guess we'll keep him."

Jim at Bat

A summer pasture at twilight:

The boy cannot hit the baseball to his satisfaction. Though he makes contact almost every time he swings the bat, he does not strike the mighty blow he sees in his mind. The ball does not leap scalded into the sky, but hops into the tall grass as if startled by a noise; it buzzes mildly, a dying beetle tied to a piece of thread, and rolls to a disappointing stop.

Uncle Zeno pitches. He tracks the ball into the grass every time the boy hits it, and retrieves it without complaint from each new hiding place. He blames himself for the boy's lack of success. The bat is simply too heavy. He knew this for fact when he bought it; he had not wanted to buy a new bat every time the boy grew an inch. He silently chides himself for being cheap.

Uncle Coran and Uncle Al man the field at improbably optimistic distances behind their brother. Their faces are indistinct in the coming darkness, their forms identical except that Uncle Coran wears a baseball glove on his left hand, while Uncle Al, who is left-handed, wears one on the right. They shout encouragement each time the boy swings the bat. They pound their fists into their gloves, though only for their nephew's benefit; their bodies no longer believe the ball will ever make it out to their place in the field. They do not creep closer because it would make the boy feel bad.

All three of the uncles wear the small, pocketless, old-fashioned baseball gloves they have had since they were boys. Uncle Al's mitt was made for a right-handed fielder, but he has worn it on the wrong hand for so long that he no longer notices that it doesn't fit. Each uncle would still gladly play a game of baseball, should anyone ask, although no one has asked for years. They keep their tiny, relic gloves properly oiled, however, as if such invitations were not only commonplace, but imminent.

The boy studies Uncle Zeno until Uncle Zeno's face seems to light up from the inside, weakly, like a moon seen through clouds. It changes into a hundred unfamiliar faces, twists into a hundred strange smiles, until the boy blinks hard and wills his eyes to see only what is there.

"Okay, Doc," Uncle Zeno says. "Keep your eye on the ball. Here it comes."

The baseball in Uncle Zeno's hand is almost invisible, a piece of smoke, a shadow. The woods on the far side of the pasture are already dark as sleep; the river twists through them by memory. Uncle Zeno tosses the ball gently toward the boy, who does not see it until its arc carries it above the black line of trees, where it hangs for a moment like an eclipse in the faintly glowing sky. The boy is arm-weary; he swings as hard as he is able. The bat and ball collide weakly. The ball drops to the ground at the boy's feet. It lies there stunned, quivering, *containing flight beneath its smooth skin. The boy switches the bat into his left hand, picks up the ball with his right, and throws it back to Uncle Zeno.*

"I hit it just about every time," the boy says.

"Batter, batter, batter, batter," Uncle Al chirps in the field.

"Say, whatta-say, whatta-say, whatta-say," chants Uncle Coran in the ancient singsong of ballplayers. The uncles are singing to the boy. He has never heard anything so beautiful. He does not want it to stop.

"Okay, Doc," says Uncle Zeno. "One more. Now watch."

BOOK II

Jim Leaves Home

The Wide Sea

JIM AND Uncle Al did not set out on their journey until after supper, when the heat of the day had broken at last, when the evening air would make traveling seem more adventure than hardship. Jim did not know where they were going, only that it was far away. Mama had packed for them a dozen ham biscuits in waxed paper, and filled a gallon jar with water. A paper bag behind the truck seat contained a pair of underwear, a pair of socks, and a clean shirt for Jim. Uncle Al had filled two vacuum bottles with black coffee, and in his pocket carried Uncle Coran's pistol. The pistol was verification of the journey's high seriousness: it usually nestled in the cash drawer at the store, and appeared, like a rare and dangerous bird, only when one of the uncles needed to shoot a snake.

Uncle Al would say only that they were going to see a man about a dog. Jim knew from experience that wasn't their true destination — there *never* was a dog — but he did not mind the mystery. He had never traveled more than thirty miles away from Aliceville in any direction; he thought he would be happy to see the sights at whatever place their travels landed them.

They passed through Shelby an hour after leaving home. For Jim, it was the point in the east beyond which lay new worlds. He had visited the town twice before, and again found it superior in every way. Unlike Aliceville, Shelby had wide, paved streets; big, painted houses with green lawns watched over them from beneath the cool shade of old trees. Downtown, Jim was surprised to see many of the stores still open for business, even as darkness approached. As they circled the courthouse, he briefly glimpsed, through an open door, the polished counter of a soda shop. Jim could no more imagine sitting inside a soda shop than in the house of a king, and did not ask Uncle Al to stop.

As they headed again into the red-hilled, open country, they passed a sign pointing the way to Charlotte. Uncle Zeno had taken Mama there one Saturday before she married Jim's father. She had bought her wedding dress in a department store. She had ridden elevators. She had almost been run down by a streetcar, which clanged past with blue electricity spitting and sparking from the wires overhead. Jim had heard the story about Mama's trip to Charlotte all his life.

He leaned over so that the warm wind whistling in through the open window blew directly into his face. When he closed one eye, the black line along the edge of the state highway disappeared into the front fender of the truck, as if the tire inside were coiling it up like a rope. When he stuck his head out of the window and looked back, he saw the line unrolling neatly behind them, marking the way they had come. They would be able to find their way home.

Small, well-tended farms, much like the ones Jim had grown up among, sat along both sides of the highway like strangers whose faces seem familiar. The farmhouses were unpainted, and sat up off the ground on red brick pillars. At the back of each house, a dim kerosene glow lit a single window. Black strings of cooking smoke uncoiled from the chimneys and disappeared into the dusky sky. Jim knew that the people who lived inside those houses were sitting down to supper and talking about the day. They worked in the cotton fields through which Jim and Uncle Al traveled. Jim studied the farms carefully; each served as last outpost along a moving frontier.

Two thoughts came to Jim at once, joined by a thread of amazement: he thought, *People live here*, and he thought, *They don't know who I am*. At that moment the world opened up around Jim like hands that, until that moment, had been cupped around him; he felt very small, almost invisible, in the open air of their center, but knew that the hands would not let him go. It was almost like flying. The expansion strips in the road bumped under the wheels of the truck in a rhythm that said, "Char-*Lotte*, Char-*Lotte*, Char-*Lotte*." The wind was rich and fragrant, familiar with the smells of dirt and fertilizer and mules, although they were a long way from the place Jim had naturally considered the source of those smells. He heard himself say out loud, "It tastes good," but Uncle Al apparently did not hear him. By the time they reached Kings Mountain, Jim was asleep.

The fierce clacking of a textile mill outside Gastonia briefly roused Jim from his slumber. The mill was three stories high, and longer than a train; the whole town of Aliceville could have fit easily inside its brick walls. It sat on the far side of an ominous, still pond, whose water disappeared without warning over the tall side of a dam. The blazing windows of the mill were reflected with alarming clarity in the pond's black water. The noise of the machines was frightening, even above the comforting grumble of the truck. Jim lay down and put his head in Uncle Al's lap. "I don't want to go in there," he said.

"I hope you don't ever have to," said Uncle Al.

By the time Jim swept his dreaming clean of noise, Uncle Al pulled on his ear. "Jim," he said, "wake up. Charlotte."

Jim rose up and tried to look. The truck floated down a peaceful river, through a deep ravine, but the ravine was filled with fog, which made it difficult to see. Trees grew thickly in the shadows along the river's banks, and dim lights hung from their branches like ripe fruit. Streetcars floated all around them. The streetcars were sound asleep, and Jim hoped the truck wouldn't wake them up.

The river smelled cool and inviting; it reminded him of rain on a road at the end of a hot day. He wanted to float down it until morning, when the fog would burn off in the sun and he could see everything. He wanted to pluck a light from a tree limb and take it home. Mama had not told him about the river and the trees and the lights; she had not told him that streetcars floated through the streets of Charlotte. From somewhere along the bank a horse spoke to him kindly.

He woke to a silence as loud as the clanging of a bell. Not until he sat up and found Uncle Al standing in the glow of the headlights, along the black edge of the world, could he hear anything at all. Uncle Al was drinking coffee and eating a ham biscuit. Beyond him lay perfect darkness, night without trees or mountains or stars, nothing to keep the sky from settling onto the ground. It had collapsed already onto the road behind them. Jim climbed out of the truck and hurried into the light. Uncle Al fished into a pocket, pulled out a biscuit, and handed it to Jim.

"Where are we?" Jim asked.

"South Carolina," said Uncle Al. "Not much to it, huh?"

"No, sir."

The air was warm and thick, a coat you couldn't take off. The light vibrated with moths; the darkness shook with the rhythmic sawing of crickets and cicadas.

"Good dirt through here, though. Can you smell it?"

"Yes, sir."

"I always did love the smell of dirt. I can tell good dirt just by smelling it. I can smell weeds, too. Did you know I could smell weeds?"

"No, sir."

"Weeds. Boll weevils. Grasshoppers. Whatever. I can smell everything."

"Yes, sir."

"I wish I could wake up, though. That's what I wish right now." Uncle Al took off his hat and hollered out into South Carolina, "OH, LORD, I WISH I COULD WAKE UP!"

They waited, but not even an echo answered back. God was asleep. It was the middle of the night. Jim giggled.

Uncle Al put his hat back on. He took another swallow of coffee and turned quickly on Jim. He said, "Do you ever wish you had a daddy?"

The words stung Jim as if they had been made of bones and meat.

"My daddy's dead," he said.

"I know, Jim," Uncle Al said. "Your daddy was a good man, and everybody wishes he was still alive. What I meant was, do you ever wish you had somebody else for a daddy?"

Nobody had ever asked Jim that before. It was not a question his mother would have allowed. He gave the idea some thought.

"No," he said finally. "I've already got three daddies."

Uncle Al stared at Jim but didn't say anything.

Jim thought he had said something wrong. "You and Uncle Zeno and Uncle Coran."

Still, Uncle Al did not respond. Uncle Al did not even appear to occupy the face that stared back at Jim.

Jim swallowed. "Boy," he said, "South Carolina sure has a lot of bugs."

Uncle Al laughed suddenly: a lone, sharp noise, like a bark.

"Let me tell you something, Jim," he said. "I don't care what anybody says. You're all right. Now eat your biscuit before I jerk a knot in your tail."

Jim woke slowly, rising through a comfortable lull of noise toward a star he realized he had been watching for some time. The truck motor droned; warm air rushed in through the window and over his cheek and whistled back out. Uncle Al was in the middle of a story whose beginning Jim already knew; Jim closed his eyes and stepped aboard as it passed:

". . . so Zeno did what Cissy asked and did not write Amos Glass until after we had buried Jim and you were born. And in the letter Zeno told Amos not to come, that Cissy was upset and not well at all and did not want to see him. But Amos, who probably never once in his life did anything somebody else told him to do, showed up at the store one afternoon right after dinner. He had hired Robley Gentine to bring him down the mountain.

"All three of us were at the store that day, we just didn't get a lot done farming that summer, and Amos comes hobbling in, old as Methuselah, using an old hoe handle like a staff, and he says, 'I'm Amos Glass. Take me to the boy.'

"And Zeno says, 'Amos, I told you in the letter that Cissy didn't want you to see the boy.'

"So Amos says right back, 'I ain't going to tell you again.'

"Now all three of us stand up then and Coran eases open the cash drawer because we don't know what's going to happen next, except that we weren't going to be pushed around on our own property, not by Amos Glass nor anybody else. But Robley Gentine, he's your great-uncle on your daddy's side, he backs up a step and says, 'Now wait a minute, boys. I ain't got no dog in this fight,' and Amos sees what the score is right quick. There was three of us and one of him and he was old. So he stares at us for a minute with those blue eyes of his, and you could see the very devil looking out, but then all of a sudden he starts to cry, just sobbing right there in the middle of the store, and he says, 'My Jimmy's gone. My Jimmy's gone. *Please* let me see the boy. *Please* let me see the boy.'

"Now, we didn't know what to do then. We knew that Cissy would kill us all if we brought Amos Glass in the house, but on the other hand the old man was so pitiful, it would just break your heart. So we told Amos to hold on and wait a minute and we went back in the storeroom and talked about it, and Coran remembered that Cissy was asleep, she slept most of the day for a long time, and we decided that maybe it wouldn't do any harm if we let Amos look in through the window.

"So we took Amos down to Zeno's, and we got a chair off the front porch, and we peeked in Cissy's window to make sure she was asleep, and then the four of us together, me and Zeno and Coran and Robley Gentine, we get Amos Glass up in that chair and we hold on to him and he looks in the window and he sees you lying there in the bed beside your Mama, it was the only time he ever saw you, and we hear him whisper, 'Jimmy, Jimmy . . .'"

And Jim smiles and steps off of the story and listens to it move out of hearing as he slips again into sleep.

The first bright sunlight of the new day found them at an abandoned country store near Florence. The small, weathered building sat hard by the highway, beneath an old oak tree with wide, spreading limbs. A single crow sat in the top of the tree, and flew away when they pulled into the lot, as if to tell someone they had come. Uncle Al drove the truck into the shade of the tree. The engine, when he turned it off, ticked hotly in the quiet morning.

The store crouched among broad, fallow fields coming up in cockleburs and broom straw and small cedar trees. Jim knew that the presence of cedar trees meant that the land was cotton ground that had been farmed too many years in a row. Now the ground was too poor to make a crop; the farmers who had tilled it were gone, and the store where the farmers shopped was closed. The uncles never planted cotton on the same ground two years in a row, and tended to look down on farmers who did.

Uncle Al took off his hat and laid it on the seat beside him.

"I'm going to take a nap," he said. "Can you keep a good lookout until I wake up?"

"Yes, sir."

"Now you better not let anything sneak up on you. If something gets a hold of me while I'm asleep, you're in big trouble."

Jim climbed out of the truck where it would be easier to keep an eye on things. He left the truck door open in case he had to get back in a hurry. The oak tree he stood beneath seemed to mark the exact center of the empty fields; the blue bowl of the sky balanced directly above it, which made the place seem important, even though nothing in the landscape, save the tree itself, suggested import. A dark line of undergrowth in the distance to the east marked the passage of a creek, but nothing else called out to the eye for notice; the old store leaned slightly toward the tree, as if dependent upon it for company.

On the porch of the store Jim found a thermometer advertising Red Rock Cola nailed like a message to the middle of the door. He studied it seriously; already it read eighty-five degrees. "It's going to be a hot one," Jim said out loud, for no other reason than to make himself brave. For all he knew, a hobo or a robber or a ghost was hiding inside the building. There was a depression on. Mama said depression made people mean. Jim tiptoed to the building's only window, sucked his lungs full of courage, and peeked through the glass. Inside was a counter made of rough lumber and a few rickety-looking shelves, but nothing else. So far, Jim thought, so good.

Behind the store he found the bleached skull of a small animal; he could find no evidence of what had killed it, and decided the culprit must have been a snake. Jim put the skull on the end of a stick and poked through the weeds around the store, but the snake evaded his searching. Twice he heard cars approaching on the highway, and both times he ran and hid behind the front of the truck, ready to wake Uncle Al, but both times the cars passed without slowing. Jim watched until they disappeared from view, just to make sure the drivers weren't trying to trick him.

In Florence, Uncle Al asked directions to the plantation of Mr. Harvey Hartsell. Mr. Hartsell had a team of matched Belgian draft horses for sale. Uncle Al had seen an ad for the horses in a farming paper. The uncles farmed with mules — they had always farmed with mules — but lately Uncle Al had begun to desire a good team of horses. He said he got tired of talking to mules all day long. Mules, said Uncle Al, weren't always truthful. Horses weren't as smart, but at least you could believe what they said.

Mr. Harvey Hartsell's place wasn't hard to find. He lived at the end of a long dirt road whose only purpose seemed to be taking travelers directly to his plantation. The house was red brick, with tall, white pillars and porches upstairs and down. It sat at the end of a long white driveway of crushed seashells. The drive was shaded by pecan trees, whose long limbs met above it; the trees formed a cool, green tunnel through which Uncle Al drove.

Jim felt suddenly ashamed of his overalls, and of the sweat ring around the crown of Uncle Al's straw hat, and of the ham biscuits they had just eaten. Mr. Harvey Hartsell's plantation did not seem to be a place they belonged. Uncle Al knocked at the tall double doors of the house for a long time. Jim was glad when no one answered.

Back at the main road, Uncle Al turned the truck toward a collection of cabins and farm buildings in the distance. The cabins they passed on the way to the main barn seemed locked up tight, although a dog slept on the porch of one, and a load of wash hung from a line in the yard of another. Uncle Al stopped beside an old truck parked in the shade of the barn. Nobody answered when he called out, but when they walked behind the barn they found an old man leaning against the whitewashed gate of a corral. Inside the corral lay two dead horses. A single buzzard sat immobile on top of each horse as if waiting for the old man to say a grace. Jim pinched his nose and held it closed. The scaly red heads of the buzzards were fierce and ugly.

"Howdy," said Uncle Al, looking at the horses.

"Howdy," said the old man.

"Are you Mr. Harvey Hartsell?"

The old man laughed as if the question was a good joke. He winked at Jim. He said, "Do I look like Mr. Harvey Hartsell to you?"

The old man didn't have any teeth. His face collapsed in on itself whenever he wasn't talking. Jim was sure Mr. Harvey Hartsell would have had teeth.

"I don't know what Harvey Hartsell looks like,"

Uncle Al said. "But you don't have to get smart about it."

Jim stared up at Uncle Al. He had never heard any of the uncles speak rudely to a stranger.

The old man, however, did not seem to notice. He tucked his thumbs into his armpits and flapped his arms up and down.

"What Harvey Hartsell looks like is a jailbird," he said. "He shot these here horses to keep the bank from gettin' 'em. He shot every animal on the place, and they locked him up."

"Good Lord," said Uncle Al.

"Everybody told me, they said, 'you better not be sneaking around Mr. Harvey Hartsell's place,' but I said, 'it ain't Mr. Harvey Hartsell's place no more, now is it? What's he going to do to *me*?'" The old man seemed pleased with the thought. He put his foot up on the lowest bar of the gate as if he owned it. "I used to work for Harvey Hartsell, but he tried to cheat me on my shares. When I called him on it, he run me off. Now he's in jail."

Jim found himself siding with Mr. Harvey Hartsell, even though Harvey Hartsell had shot the horses Uncle Al had come all this way to see.

"Them horses," said the old man, "was *Belgiums*."

"Belgians," said Uncle Al.

He leaned over and climbed through the bars of the gate and walked slowly across the corral. One of the buzzards grabbed onto the air with its great wings and flew heavily across the fields. The other buzzard, however, raised its wings and hissed at Uncle Al. The sun shone through its feathers. Jim would have found the wings beautiful, had they

not been attached to the buzzard's lizard head.
Uncle Al stopped, pulled the pistol out of his
pocket, and pointed it at the bird.

"Uh-oh," said the old man. "Time to go." He
hurried stiffly around the side of the barn, holding
on to his hat.

Jim let go of his nose and stuck his fingers in his
ears. After a second he thought better of it and
pinched his nose shut again. The shot wasn't as
loud as he thought it would be: it sounded flat and
thin in the heat, and did not make an echo. The
buzzard folded its wings carefully into place and
fell sleepily off the horse. A thin veil of flies rose
above the horse for a moment, in what seemed to
Jim the shape of a horse, but quickly settled back
down. Uncle Al replaced the pistol in his pocket
and walked over to where the horses lay. Jim had
not realized how big they were until he saw Uncle
Al standing beside them. They had been immense
animals, bigger than any mule he had ever seen.
They looked like they could have pulled the barn
down, had Uncle Al been able to coax them up
and into harness. Uncle Al looked down at the
dead horses a long time. He did not seem to mind
the smell.

Instead of heading back to Aliceville, Uncle Al
drove from Florence toward Myrtle Beach. He said
he had never seen the ocean, and thought that he
might as well take a look. This was unusual behav-
ior, because Uncle Al had work to do back home.
But the change of plan suited Jim fine: he had
never seen the ocean either.

The highway they followed soon dove down into the coastal lowland. In many places dark, still water lay on both sides of the road. Gnarled, gray trees stuck up out of the water, and long snakes of moss hung down from their limbs. The swamps were drained by black rivers, choked with snags, whose waters did not seem to move at all. It took a long time to pass through such places, and Jim was glad they didn't stop. When the road rose up out of the swamps, it wandered through small settlements of dilapidated cabins. The yards of the cabins were filled with chickens and small, dirty children. Packs of dogs of all colors and sizes flew viciously from underneath their porches and gamely chased the truck, snapping at its tires. Near each settlement lay wide bottoms of cotton and tobacco, where field hands in straw hats or bright head rags stared up from the rows as the strange truck passed. Occasionally they spied large, white houses, set back in the trees, far back from the road. Jim wondered if the bank would get these places, too, and if their owners would stalk through their barns and pastures, killing everything in sight. For the first time since leaving Aliceville, Jim found himself longing for home. He was glad he didn't live in South Carolina.

Eventually they drove out of the swamps and plantations and entered a desolate barren in which there was nothing at all to see except pine trees. When they crossed finally out of the pines, they discovered the wide sea. Jim's breath caught up in his throat like it was afraid to come out. He tried to breathe several times, but drew no air. He wished that just for a moment, until he grew used to the sight, the ocean would simply *hold still*. But the waves lined up and bore down on the wide, white beach like a gang of boys intent on jumping a gully. Each wave rose up and took a running go and rushed toward South Carolina and cast itself down on the sand. And each wave when it crashed and broke sounded to Jim like the angry breath of God.

"Well, there it is," said Uncle Al.

"There it is," said Jim.

"The Atlantic Ocean."

"Yes, sir."

"It's amazing a man can live his whole life and never think about something that big."

"Yes, sir."

"I guess we studied it in school, but I don't remember. I don't remember the last time I thought about the ocean."

"No, sir."

"But there it is."

"Yes, sir."

They got out of the truck and started down the dune toward the beach. The dune was covered with a type of oats that rattled in the wind from the sea. Uncle Al stopped and studied them closely; Jim stood first on one foot and then the other and paid the oats no attention at all. The sand was burning his feet. Once they reached the beach the sand was cooler, but the roar of the water was fiercer than it had been up on the dune. Jim could taste the salty water, broken up and falling through the air. He reached up and grabbed Uncle Al's hand.

"We probably shouldn't get in that water, Jim," Uncle Al said. "We don't know anything about that water."

"I'm not going to," said Jim.

They stopped well short of the dark line on the sand that marked the farthest approach of the sea. They looked for a while at the place in the distance where the blue sky and the blue water became the same thing. At the edge of the surf a small white bird with long legs ran up and down. It ran up the slope of the beach toward the dune when the waves came in, and toward the water when they went back out. It seemed to be looking for something it could not find in the dangerous place where the water stopped and the land began. When they got too close, it flew away, crying out "kee-kee-kee-kee."

"Jim," said Uncle Al, "I just want you to know that we don't owe anybody anything. We pay as we go. Do you understand that?"

"Yes, sir."

"I just wanted you to know."

"Yes, sir."

Jim thought for a minute and pointed at the ocean. "Is our river in there?"

"Somewhere," said Uncle Al, "but I'd hate to have to hunt for it."

"Me too," said Jim. He thought for a moment more and said, "Does the ocean touch Belgium?"

"For a little ways, I think," said Uncle Al.

"Why did you shoot that buzzard?"

"I don't know. I just couldn't stand to see a buzzard standing on a horse."

"Oh," said Jim.

"I shouldn't have, I don't guess. He was just doing what buzzards do."

"It's okay, Uncle Al."

"Don't ever make fun of the misfortune of others, Jim."

"I won't."

"No good will ever come of it. God will bring you down. If you use his blessings to look down on other people, it's like cussing. It's like taking his name in vain. Do you understand that?"

"Yes, sir."

Uncle Al took off his hat and wiped his face with the back of his sleeve. "It's been a long trip, hasn't it, Jim?"

"Yes, sir."

"I'm about ready to go home and stay there. You want to get in that water first?"

"No."

"I think we should."

"I don't want to."

"Just a little ways," said Uncle Al. "I won't let it get you. That way, when we get back home we can tell Zeno and Coran that we got in the Atlantic Ocean."

Uncle Al took off his shoes and socks and dropped them onto the sand. He rolled up the legs of his overalls and led Jim to the edge of the sea, where a wave, and then another, slid up over their ankles. The water was warmer than Jim had imagined it would be. A fish no bigger than a thought swam by his feet; when he wiggled his toes it vanished as if made of light. In the water he could feel the river that flowed through the uncles' fields. Maybe Uncle Zeno or Uncle Coran had looked at the river that morning. Maybe they had wet a bandanna in its water and wiped the sweat off their faces. Jim held on to Uncle Al's hand and closed his eyes and tried to feel Belgium. He tried until he grew dizzy and felt the water writing strange words on his feet. But when he opened his eyes all he saw was ocean, the strong water rearing up.

"I wish we could've got there sooner," Uncle Al said.

"Me too," said Jim.

BOOK III

Town Boys
and Mountain Boys

First Day

THE MORNING smelled like school.

The previous morning had smelled only like summer, like dew and grass and crops growing in the fields. But this morning the air bore the suggestion of books and pencils and chalky erasers, the promised end of the long, slow days. During breakfast the delicious, new air tickled Jim's lungs. Things were going to move faster now, he could tell. He drained the last few swallows of milk from his glass and pushed himself away from the table.

"Well," he said, as matter-of-factly as possible, "I guess I better be getting to school."

At that Mama and the uncles slid their chairs away from the table and stood up.

"I'll get my hat," said Uncle Al.

"I'll do the dishes when we get home," said Mama.

"It won't hurt anything if the store opens a little late," said Uncle Coran.

"Okay, then," said Uncle Zeno, "we best be on our way."

"Wait a minute," Jim said. "Where are y'all going?"

Uncle Zeno looked confused. "We're going to school. With you."

"With me?" Jim sputtered. "Why are you going to school with me?"

"We want to meet your teacher," said Uncle Al.

"And see your classroom," said Mama.

"And meet all your little friends," said Uncle Coran.

Jim stared up at them in horror. Not even first graders were accompanied to school by their whole families. He could see himself walking up into the school yard, trailed by his mother and his uncles, as if they were a pack of dogs who would not go back to the house when he told them. He could hear all the kids at the new school, hundreds of them, laughing at him. He flushed just thinking about it.

Now Uncle Zeno looked hurt.

"What's the matter, Doc?" he said. "Don't you want us to go to school with you?"

Jim looked from face to face, his mouth open. He didn't want to hurt their feelings, but he didn't want them to go to school with him, either. After all, he was in the fourth grade now.

But before he could say anything, a single, bird-like titter escaped from Mama's mouth. And then Uncle Coran, who had obviously been holding his breath, snorted like a pig. When Uncle Zeno and Uncle Al began to shake, Jim knew that they had never intended to accompany him to school. In a moment he was lost amid the uncles, who swarmed around the table and hustled him to the door, their voices combining into a single, unintelligible din of laughter and teasing. Mama handed him his notebook and his ball glove as the uncles jostled him across the porch and down the steps.

When Jim reached the state highway, he turned and looked back. Mama and the uncles waved from the porch.

"Be good, Doc," called Uncle Zeno.

"Study hard," said Mama.

"Pay attention," said Uncle Al.

"Don't get a paddling," said Uncle Coran.

"'Bye," yelled Jim, waving back. "'Bye, everybody."

And when he turned and looked up the hill toward the school, he wished for a moment that he did not have to take another step, that he could stay right where he was and never have to leave again.

Jim had never seen so many kids in one place in his life. The students from the five smaller schools the new school replaced — first graders through high school seniors — surrounded him in the school yard. At first, Jim did not see anyone he knew. But then Buster Burnette, a fourth grader from the old school, found him in the crowd, and together they located Crawford Wilson, also from their school, and Larry Lawter, who was Buster's cousin and whom Jim knew from church, and Larry's friend Dennis Deane, with whom Larry had gone to school in Sunny View. Together the five boys formed a gang sizable enough to stand together in the school yard without having to be afraid of bigger boys.

Jim was happy to be surrounded by so many boys. Most days during the summer he never saw another kid. He was pleased when the other boys began to ask him what they should do and where they should go, as if they had met secretly before he got there and elected him leader.

Jim already knew that he was a better ballplayer than Buster and Crawford, and knew that he could outrun them as well. He sized up Larry Lawter, who was too fat to be very fast, and Dennis Deane, who was small, and figured he could outrun both of them, too. He also noticed that he was taller than the other boys. Not that he would have used his size to bully them. He was the boy the other boys looked up to, and took the responsibilities of his office seriously. He told them he thought they should try to have a ball game during recess. Each boy in turn admired Jim's glove and tried it on. They pounded their fists into the pocket and snapped it, like a crawdad's claw, at imaginary baseballs.

At exactly eight o'clock, the new principal, Mr. Dunlap, walked out of the front door and, simply by raising his arms like Moses, silenced the great crowd of students milling around the steps. Starting with the first-grade teacher, a pretty woman named Miss Lathan, he introduced the teachers one at a time and read a list of the kids who would be in their classes. Those kids then lined up and followed their teachers into the building.

The fourth-grade teacher was a short, plump

older woman named Miss Nanney. She had a perfectly round belly and curly hair that wasn't quite gray, but not quite any other color, either. Before Mr. Dunlap even finished reading the fourth-grade roll, she snapped her fingers and pointed at Jim and his friends for giggling in line, which made them want to giggle even more. Mr. Dunlap looked at them sternly when they marched past him into the building.

"Boy," Buster whispered into Jim's ear. "This is going to be the best year."

Because Miss Nanney's classroom, like the rest of the unfinished school, lacked a ceiling, it had an open, barnlike feel. The walls, however, were freshly plastered and newly painted white, decorated with large, colorful maps of the United States, the Confederacy, and the Holy Land during the time of Jesus. The floors gleamed beneath a fragrant coat of linseed oil. The blackboard had never been written on. Almost all of one wall was taken up by tall windows that reached from the ceiling to the floor; the room was bright despite the fact that, until the power lines reached Aliceville, the electric lights would not work. Jim found the room altogether satisfactory.

The first thing Miss Nanney did was seat Jim and his friends as far away from one another as possible, so that they would not get into mischief together during class. She sat Jim down in the front row, which suited him fine. Jim had always liked school, and liked to be at the front of the class. He already yearned for an assignment so he could prove to Miss Nanney how smart he was.

"I guess you've noticed there are a lot of empty desks in this classroom," Miss Nanney said after she finished assigning seats.

Miss Nanney had not been in favor of school consolidation, and had left the small school in High Shoals only grudgingly.

"There are empty seats in this room because the bus from Lynn's Mountain has yet to make it here. And if the bus from Lynn's Mountain can't make it on time during a dry September, I have no idea how it will fare during the winter. I will therefore wait to call the roll."

Jim swiveled around and looked behind him at the empty desks. He hadn't noticed before how there were no kids from Lynn's Mountain in Miss Nanney's class. Although the base of Lynn's Mountain wasn't that far from Aliceville, a trip to the top, because of the narrow, twisting roads, constituted a considerable journey. Jim wondered if the boys from the mountain would be more like his father, who by all accounts had been a kind and gentle man, or if they would be more like his grandfather, who was famously mean. And he wondered if these new boys would recognize the name Jim Glass, if he would have to fight them on the playground because he was related to a mean man he had never met.

When recess came at ten o'clock, Jim took the bat and ball Miss Nanney produced from a closet and adjourned with the boys to the new chicken-wire backstop at the far corner of the playground. They agreed unanimously that asking the girls to play ball was out of the question. The girls stayed near the building and jumped rope. Because the boys numbered only five, Jim suggested that they play roll-the-bat instead of a regular ball game.

Before they could even start, however, Crawford Wilson spotted Miss Nanney coming around the side of the building with five boys and four girls. She stopped at the edge of the playground and pointed first at the girls jumping rope, and then she pointed across the playground toward the backstop.

"Who's that?" Buster Burnette asked as the new boys walked toward them.

"I bet they're the kids from Lynn's Mountain," Jim said.

"Hillbillies," said Dennis Deane, which made everybody snicker uneasily. Nobody mentioned that the new boys were dressed in overalls exactly like theirs.

The new boys seemed to be led by a tall, handsome boy with inky black hair and dark eyes. He stopped directly in front of Jim, while the other new boys gathered around him. He was about Jim's height, or maybe a hair taller. Jim thought he looked smug and bossy.

"I'm Penn Carson," the new boy said to Jim in a slightly odd accent.

"I'm Jim Glass," said Jim. "These are my friends."

He introduced them, while the new boys looked them over. Penn Carson nodded and pointed at his friends.

"This is Otis Shehan. And Mackey MacDowell and Willie McBee and Horace Gentine."

Everybody mumbled "hey" all around.

"I think we might be some kind of cousins," Horace Gentine said to Jim.

"I don't think I have any cousins," Jim said. He didn't know if he did or not.

"I know who your granddaddy is," said Otis Shehan.

Jim studied Otis. He was a lot smaller than Jim, but he looked mean.

"I don't have anything to do much with my granddaddy," said Jim.

"Your name is Penn?" Buster Burnette said to the new boy.

"I'm named for William Penn. He was the founder of Pennsylvania. My mother was a Quaker missionary from Philadelphia. She was the teacher at our school until it closed."

Penn spoke schoolteacher English, which made Jim a little self-conscious.

"What's a Quaker?" Crawford Wilson asked.

"It's pretty complicated," Willie McBee said.

"It's a form of Christianity," said Penn.

"It ain't Baptist," Larry Lawter said.

"Or Methodist," said Buster Burnette.

"It's a Yankee religion," said Dennis Deane, but nobody laughed.

"Penn ain't a Yankee," Otis Shehan said. "And *he* won't fight because it's against his religion."

Penn held out his hand, as if to keep Otis from saying more.

"I was born in North Carolina, just like y'all," he said.

"Miss Nanney says we're supposed to play ball," said Horace Gentine. "Are we going to play ball, or are we gonna talk?"

"How about us against y'all?" Jim said. "The town boys against the mountain boys." The two teams regarded each other warily. Nobody knew what to say.

Penn finally nodded. "Okay," he said.

The town boys batted first and scored twelve runs. Jim got on base all three times he came up to bat. Larry Lawter, who not only couldn't run very fast, but couldn't bat very well, either, made all three of the outs. When the mountain boys came up, Jim saw quickly that the town boys had their hands full. Otis Shehan, Mackey MacDowell, and Horace Gentine loaded the bases before Penn came to the plate and swatted a ball to center that rolled almost all the way across the playground before Buster Burnette could run it down. Penn homered again the next time he came to the plate, this time to right field, with two runners on. Between pitches, Jim began to watch Miss Nanney, hoping that she would call them in before the mountain boys tied the score. But she stood placidly in the shade of the building, apparently in no hurry to return to the classroom.

Penn came to the plate a third time with two outs, the bases loaded, and the mountain boys down by three. Jim looked at Miss Nanney, who still showed no signs of ending the rally. On the first pitch Jim threw, Penn socked a long line drive to left field. Crawford, who was playing deep, chased after it. Jim ran to shortstop to cut off the relay throw. Dennis ran home to cover the plate.

Jim fielded Crawford's throw and turned just in time to see Penn rounding third. He saw that Penn would reach home before his throw would. He threw the ball as hard as he could and it hit Penn between the shoulder blades, knocking him to the ground just as he touched the plate. Jim didn't know in his own heart if he had hit Penn on purpose or not.

Penn scrambled up and twirled toward Jim, his face flushed with anger, his fists balled at his sides. Jim threw down his glove and got ready to fight.

The town boys and the mountain boys looked at Jim in disbelief. They stood still and watched to see what would happen. Jim had never seen anybody angrier than Penn. Still, Penn did not move forward. Across the playground, Miss Nanney raised her arm in the air, signaling the end of recess.

"That was dirty," Otis Shehan said.

"Did you do that on purpose?" Penn asked.

"It was an accident," Jim said. "I promise."

Penn unclenched his fists. He brushed the dirt off of his overalls.

"Mountain boys thirteen, town boys twelve," Jim said, trying to smile. "We better go in."

He picked up his glove and turned toward the school. On the way back across the playground, he walked by himself. Not even the town boys knew what to say to him.

Big Day

JIM DID not sleep much the night before Big Day. The idea of the new school's open house itself had not kept him awake, but the small carnival waiting on the playground had driven him to distraction. He was up and dressed and through with breakfast by seven, even though it was a Saturday. He paced back and forth between the front porch and the kitchen, huffing with impatience. He was afraid that Penn might get to the school before he did; he was afraid that Penn would ride the rides first.

In the three weeks since the start of term, Jim and Penn had turned the school yard into their own private arena. They raced across the playground when recess started, and raced back when it was over. When Penn volunteered to wash the blackboard, Jim offered to beat the erasers. Penn memorized more Bible verses than Jim, but Jim won the spelling bee. When Miss Nanney set the class to work painting pictures of Bible scenes with which to decorate the walls for Big Day, Jim and Penn each painted a picture of David slaying Goliath; each then begged Miss Nanney to judge which one was best.

From the front porch Jim could see the merry-go-round and the Ferris wheel. In the kitchen Uncle Zeno said, "No, Doc, it's not time to go yet." From the front porch, he could see the tall, skinned poplar log that had been sunk into the ground for the greasy pole–climbing contest. In the kitchen Mama said, "Jim, you are worrying me to death."

Big Day started at ten o'clock, when Mr. Dunlap would unlock the school doors. Mama did not seem to care that cars and trucks already lined the school driveway, that everybody and their brother was coming in from the countryside by the truckload, by the wagonload, and on foot, to see the new building and ride the rides; she did not seem to care that they would take up all the shady places to put their dinner on the ground. She especially did not care that Penn Carson might get in line for the Ferris wheel before Jim did.

By eight o'clock, Jim did not see how he could live two more hours.

By eight-thirty, Uncle Zeno had had enough. He slapped his leg with the *Progressive Farmer* he had been trying to read.

"Come on, Doc," he said. "We're going for a walk."

"I don't want to go for a walk," Jim said.

"Ain't no 'want to' about it," said Uncle Zeno.

*   *   *

Uncle Zeno strode through the pastures and the fields as if he were on his way to something important, and not away from it. Jim followed at a distance great enough to show his displeasure, but not great enough to get himself in trouble. He tried not to enjoy how good the morning sun felt on his back; he tried to ignore the sweet air on his face.

They crossed the creek on the stepping-stones, passed through the walnut grove, and came into the big corn bottom. The corn that had been knee-high to the uncles and the field hands in June was now seven and eight feet tall. It was still green, but thin, brown stripes, like those found on garter snakes, were beginning to darken the edges of the long leaves. Each stalk was topped by an elaborate, tasseled headdress; each heavy ear sprouted a protruding mane of silk. When Jim and Uncle Zeno walked through the field, the leaves whispered that fall was coming.

On the far side of the bottom, they passed out of the corn and into the ribbon of tangled woods that marked the passage of the river. They carefully followed a narrow path through the poison oak. With each step, the river-smell grew stronger; the gurgling sound of water seeking its way through smooth, flat rocks grew louder. The path ended at the wide, flat rock from which the uncles liked to fish. Beyond the rock, the river bent suddenly toward South Carolina, as if intent on leaving their country for good. This was the place that for Jim marked the boundary of home; on the far side of the river lay another place entirely.

Uncle Zeno hopped from the bank onto the rock. Jim followed him and sat down near the water. The rock had been warmed by the sun, but the air near the water raised gooseflesh on his arms. Jim stared at the green water; he lay back and stared at the blue sky. He wondered what was going on in town. He thought jealously of not just Penn, but of all the kids who would get to the school before he did.

"You got ants in your britches today, don't you, Doc?" Uncle Zeno said.

Jim didn't say anything. If he had been at Big Day, he would have been in line for the Ferris wheel first.

"Don't worry," Uncle Zeno said. "It'll be Big Day all day."

"How many people do you think will be at Big Day?" Jim asked.

"Oh, I don't know," said Uncle Zeno. "The weather's good. Several hundred, I reckon."

"Do you think it will be the most people to ever be in Aliceville at one time?"

"Hmm," Uncle Zeno said. "I hadn't thought about that. Could be."

"More than when Alice came?" Alice was the little girl for whom the town had been named.

"I don't know. There were a lot of folks in town that day. That was a big day, too."

"How old were you when Alice came?"

"Five," said Uncle Zeno. "You sure you want to hear this again?"

Jim nodded, and for the first time all morning began to think of something other than Big Day.

*   *   *

"Well, this happened during the last century," Uncle Zeno said, glancing slyly at Jim.

He always began stories that happened before he was seven years old by saying, "This happened during the last century."

"Little Corrie and Little Allie hadn't come along yet, nor your mother, and I was the only little fellow running around the place. Now, my granddaddy (that's your great-granddaddy) and my daddy (your granddaddy, who died in 1918 with the flu) were doing pretty well. They were farming in a big way and they had the gin and the store and the mill and business was going good, and there was a tannery here then, and the tannery ran a big crew, and a sawmill, and Abraham and his bunch lived up on the hill, and it started to look to everybody like they lived in a regular town. Only they knew it wasn't a real town because they couldn't get the train to stop. You could flag it down, but if the flag wasn't out, it went on through without even slowing down. And Granddaddy hated to see that. Everybody knows you ain't got much of a town if a railroad track runs through it but the train won't stop.

"So one day Granddaddy packs a bag and flags the train down and goes to see the superintendent down in Hamlet and asks him if he'll make the train stop. But the superintendent, he says, 'My train only stops in towns. You can flag the train down like the rest of the country folk.'

"Granddaddy comes back home, and he drives a big, iron stake right in the middle of town and he surveys out a half a mile from that stake in every direction, which made a circle a mile wide, and he gets everybody who owns property inside that circle to sign a petition, and he takes that survey and that petition all the way to Raleigh and files articles of incorporation. Then he goes to Hamlet and he says, 'Now, look here. We got a town. We got a survey. We got articles of incorporation.'

"But the superintendent, he says, 'I don't care about your articles of incorporation. You ain't got a depot for the train to stop at.'

"So Granddaddy, who by now is getting kind of aggravated at the superintendent, comes back home and with his own money builds a depot right over the top of that stake, beside the railroad track, in the dead center of town. Then he goes back to the superintendent one more time and he says, 'All right. I made you a town. I built you a depot. If you'll make the train stop, I'll *give* that depot to the railroad.'

"Now, Aliceville, as you know, was at that time called Sandy Bottom. That's just what it had always been called. So the superintendent, who wasn't too crazy about Granddaddy, either, he says, 'I don't care how many depots you give me, my train ain't stopping at no place called Sandy Bottom.'

"Granddaddy comes back home and he thinks about it, and he decides that maybe this time the superintendent has a point. Sandy Bottom ain't much of a name for a town. So he asks around to see if anybody can think up a name, but nobody couldn't think of anything good, nothing anyway that would stop a train.

"Now, the engineer of the train at that time was a fellow named Bill McKinney. He was raised not far from here, down a little ways on the other side of the river, and his people still lived around. He was a big old handsome fellow with big waxed mustaches, and he was proud of that train. And the only thing he was prouder of than that train was his little girl, Alice. And everybody knew that.

"So one Sunday in church, Granny (that's your great-grandmother), it came to her that all this time Granddaddy had been talking to the wrong man. She thought that maybe instead of working on the man who was in *charge* of the train — but lived all the way down in Hamlet — they ought to work on the man who *drove* the train and came through here every day. She's the one who thought up the name Aliceville.

"Now Granddaddy thought that was a pretty smart idea, even if he didn't think of it. He talked it around and everybody else agreed that it was a pretty good name for a town — everybody liked Bill McKinney, you see — and anyway it was better than Sandy Bottom. So Granddaddy painted 'Aliceville' on a sign and climbed up on a ladder and nailed it to the side of the depot. It's the same one that's up there today.

"Now Bill McKinney, when he heard about what was going on from his people, he didn't believe it. The first time the train came through after Granddaddy put the sign up, he stopped and climbed down out of the cab to take a look. And, big as he was, Bill McKinney almost broke down crying when he saw it, he loved Alice so much. He told

Granddaddy that as far as he was concerned, the flag was always out at Aliceville, and he was going to stop the train every day, going and coming, no matter what the superintendent said.

"Things went on that way for a while, the train stopping twice a day even though it wasn't supposed to, and one thing led to another, and pretty soon the superintendent gave in and put Aliceville on the regular schedule. Oh, that was good news. Everybody in town got together and planned a celebration, because now Aliceville was an official town, as much as Shelby or New Carpenter or Charlotte or New York City, and they asked Bill McKinney if he would bring Alice.

"The celebration was set for a Sunday, and the train made a special run. Everybody came in from the country and brought their dinner and stayed the day. They had mule races and footraces and sack races and three-legged races and a greased-pig chase, and they had a greasy pole–climbing contest — which I didn't do no good at, I was too small — and sometime in the middle of the afternoon we heard the train whistle, and we looked and saw the smoke coming in the distance, and everybody ran down to the depot. When the train came up to the depot and stopped, it was all shined up, and it had flags and banners hung all over it, and Alice McKinney, the girl they had named the town after, was up in the cab with her mama and her daddy. She must have been six or seven, just a little older than I was.

"Lord, Jim, I can still see her. She was wearing a

white dress and a little crown, and I thought she was the prettiest thing I had ever seen, standing up there in the cab and waving at everybody. We cheered and cheered. Granddaddy had covered the Aliceville sign on the side of the depot with a sheet, and Alice got down off the train with her mama and daddy and pulled a rope and the sheet came down and everybody cheered again. I was just five years old then, and I thought that was the grandest day there had ever been. I thought Alice McKinney was like a queen or a princess, something out of a picture book, and I couldn't believe I was standing there looking at her. Everybody was so happy. Town seemed like a different place. It finally seemed like *somewhere*.

"But, one day not long after that, the train came through and Bill McKinney wasn't driving it. A substitute man was. And the substitute man got down and told us that Alice had come down sick. She had the whooping cough or diphtheria, I don't remember which. And as long as she was sick, people waited for that whistle, and when the substitute man pulled in, everybody stopped what they were doing and went down to the depot to see how Alice was. And every day he told us she was getting a little worse, that she was sinking a little lower. Women from here started frying chickens and making pies and cakes and sending them back with the substitute man.

"Then one day we heard the train whistle start up way outside of town, long before it got to the crossing, just a continuous blast, and it got louder and louder, and it didn't let up, and everybody ran fast as they could down to the track to see what was wrong. I remember running down the street holding Mama's hand. Well, the train didn't stop that day. When it came through, it was going so fast and the whistle was so loud, you could feel the ground shake. I'd never seen a train go that fast. And in the instant it flashed by, we could see that Bill McKinney was driving. He was staring straight ahead. He didn't look left nor right, and he had this awful look on his face, and that's when we knew that Alice had died.

"That was the last we ever saw of Bill McKinney in this country. Seeing that sign on the side of the depot pained him so much that he got off the train at New Carpenter and refused to get back on it. They had to send a man all the way from Hamlet to drive it back. They say Bill McKinney walked all the way back home overland, staying on the other side of the river to keep away from Aliceville. He and his wife packed up and moved away from here, and he got a job driving trains in Oklahoma or somewhere, that's what his people said, and if he ever came back through this country, I never heard of it.

"Everybody felt just awful, and nobody knew what to do. They talked about changing the name back to Sandy Bottom, or changing it to something else, but that just didn't seem right. They worried about how it would make Bill McKinney feel if they changed it, and they worried that it would dishonor Alice, which nobody wanted to do. But at the same time, not changing it didn't seem like much of a bargain, either, because the sign reminded everybody of what had happened. So nobody did anything, and the sign stayed up on the side of the depot, and after a while people stopped thinking about it, which is just how people are.

"But let me tell you something, Jim. It don't happen every day, it don't happen every week, but there's still days that hearing that train whistle makes me remember how I felt looking up at Alice that one time. And I remember the awful look on Bill McKinney's face. I'm forty-three years old now, and all this happened thirty-seven, thirty-eight years ago, but sometimes I can see it just as clear."

Jim lay back on the rock, his face covered with his arm, pretending to be bothered by the sun.

"Oh, well," Uncle Zeno said, patting Jim on the leg. "That was a long time ago."

Jim rubbed his eyes with the heels of his hands.

"How old would Alice be now if she hadn't died?" he asked.

"I don't know. Forty-four, forty-five, not too old, just a little older than I am."

"Do you think you would have married her?"

Uncle Zeno looked startled. "What in the world kind of question is that?" he said.

"I don't know," said Jim. "I was just wondering if you would have married Alice if she hadn't died."

"I never met Alice. What made you think of that?"

Jim shrugged. "Whenever you tell that story, I just wish you could have married Alice."

Uncle Zeno looked off somewhere and smiled.

"Well, you know, Doc," he said. "Just between me and you, I wish I could have, too."

"Why didn't you and Uncle Coran and Uncle Al ever get married?"

"I don't know. I guess a man can get too busy when marrying time comes, or there might not be enough girls to go around for everybody. Before you know it you get locked in to what you're doing and you just keep doing it. It's best not to think about it too much. You ready to go back?"

An Unexpected Guest

WHEN JIM and Uncle Zeno walked in the back door, Jim knew something was wrong. Jim thought at first that they had stayed away too long, but when Mama furrowed her brow slightly at Uncle Zeno and tilted her head toward Uncle Al's house Jim knew it had nothing to do with them.

Jim followed Uncle Zeno out onto the front porch, where they found Uncle Coran sitting on the steps, cleaning his fingernails with a knife. Uncle Coran whistled in a descending tone, like a bomb falling, and pointed with his chin toward Uncle Al's. Uncle Al was sitting on his porch with Whitey Whiteside. Uncle Al and Whitey Whiteside looked over at them and waved.

"What's going on?" Jim asked.

Everybody seemed as if they were about to laugh at a joke he didn't quite understand.

"It looks like Whitey Whiteside is going to go to Big Day with us, is all," Uncle Zeno said. "Is that all right with you?"

Jim didn't know what he was supposed to say. He shrugged and watched the Ferris wheel turning on top of the hill. It didn't seem so urgent that he ride it now, although he couldn't say why.

"Let's shake a leg, then," said Uncle Zeno.

Jim led the way up the hill to the school, lugging the peach basket that held their lunch. With each step he took, the basket banged against his leg like a drum. Behind Jim, Mama walked between Uncle Coran and Uncle Zeno, clinging tightly to their arms. Uncle Al and Whitey Whiteside brought up the rear about ten yards farther back. Uncle Al carried a gallon jar of tea in the crook of his arm as if it were a baby.

"What I want to know," Mama said in a low voice, "is whose idea was it?"

"I don't know what you're talking about," said Uncle Coran.

"You do too know what I'm talking about, Coran McBride."

"Hush," said Uncle Zeno.

Jim looked over his shoulder at Mama. He didn't recognize the look on her face. She didn't quite look mad, although she didn't quite look as if she wasn't mad, either.

"Is there something wrong with your nose, Doc?" Uncle Zeno said.

"No, sir," Jim said, pointing it again up the hill. The red school loomed above them. The wide doors were propped open; the yard was alive with people.

"I will not be made a fool of," Mama said. "I will not be ganged up on and humiliated in public."

"Oh, Cissy," Uncle Coran said softly, "it's nothing like that."

"What's it like then?" Mama asked. "Tell me, Coran."

Jim turned around and marched backward up the hill. The uncles looked grim. Whitey Whiteside looked frightened. Mama blinked wetly. It came to Jim then that Mama was upset because Whitey Whiteside was going with them to Big Day. And once he wondered why Whitey Whiteside's presence would upset Mama, other questions began pulling into his head like trains into a station. Only none of the questions had words, only empty places, followed by empty places where answers should have been. They rushed past him like pieces of fog, things he could see but could not grab. Eventually a huge question began to take shape inside his chest and fill itself with air. He opened his mouth to say something, but did not know exactly what.

But before Jim could speak, Uncle Zeno narrowed his eyes at him and pointed up the hill with his free arm.

"You better turn around and watch where you're going, Doc," he said.

"Hush, you two," he said to Mama and Uncle Coran. "The corn has ears."

"Jim and I have already had a look around up here," Whitey Whiteside said when they reached the school yard. "Haven't we, Jim?"

"Have you?" said Mama without looking at Whitey Whiteside.

"On his birthday," Whitey said. "Isn't that right, Jim?"

When Jim looked around to answer, nobody seemed to be paying him any attention. Whitey swallowed uncomfortably. Uncle Zeno took the dinner basket from Jim. Jim led everybody up the wide steps and into the building, which in less than a month had already acquired the chalk and book smell it would always keep. The hallway was crowded. The school still didn't have ceilings, and most of the people stared up at the thick joists that supported the second floor. The exposed joists were an unexpected, disquieting sight, like bones in a field. Thick steam pipes for the radiators bored through the joists in straight lines and turned suddenly in sharp elbows. Black wires wrapped on porcelain insulators snaked among the steam pipes, waiting for the day the electricity would come. The dead light fixtures hung down from the wires like unlit moons. Above the joists and the pipes and the wires, vague shadows passed back and forth as people walked over the floorboards upstairs. Here and there a flooring nail that had missed a joist poked angrily through a nest of long splinters. Staring up with Mama and the uncles, Jim was embarrassed that his school didn't have ceilings, although he had never felt that way before, had never thought much about it one way or the other.

"Goodness," Mama said. "I hope they finish it soon."

"It looks okay to me," said Uncle Coran, who made a show of studying the floor.

"My room's this way," Jim said, pointing down the oiled hallway.

Miss Nanney sat behind her desk as she always did, her posture perfect, as it always was. Jim looked at her and wondered if she ever went home.

"Hello, Jim Glass," she said gruffly, looking at him over her glasses as if the two of them shared a secret, which she was about to tell.

"Hey, Miss Nanney," Jim said, looking at his feet.

Mama and the uncles introduced themselves to Miss Nanney and shook her hand.

"And who is this?" Miss Nanney said, peering around Uncle Al at Whitey Whiteside.

"This is Whitey Whiteside," Uncle Zeno said. "A friend of the family."

"A friend of my brothers," said Mama.

"I see," said Miss Nanney.

"I travel for Governor Feeds," Whitey said, a little loudly.

Uncle Coran ruffled Jim's hair.

"Miss Nanney," he said, "tell us about this knothead right here."

Uncle Coran had never ruffled Jim's hair before. Jim made a face.

"Jim Glass," Miss Nanney said with a dramatic pause, "is a pretty good boy. Sometimes, though, I am tempted to thump his ears."

"You thump 'em if he needs it," Uncle Zeno said.

"Thump both of 'em," said Uncle Al.

"Thump 'em good," said Uncle Coran.

"He is, however, mostly a good citizen."

"Good citizenship is important," said Whitey

Whiteside. Then he blushed, excused himself, and left the room.

"Who was that again?" Miss Nanney asked.

"A friend of ours," said Uncle Al.

"A traveling salesman," said Mama.

"Miss Nanney," Uncle Zeno said, "it was a pleasure to meet you."

Puzzled, Miss Nanney looked from one face to another, trying to figure out what she had just missed. She fluttered to her feet like a plump bird.

"Oh," she said. "Likewise. Likewise I'm *sure*."

News from the Mountain

AFTER THE picnic dinner, Jim grew tired of riding the Ferris wheel, and tired of listening to the uncles talk with other men about politics and weather and crops and dogs; he grew tired of chasing boys who were younger than he was, and running from boys who were older; he grew tired of pretending that he wasn't showing off when he knew the girls were watching.

He climbed the side steps into the school building, which seemed cool and empty and quiet, and left the noise and excitement of Big Day outside. The low sun at his back gleamed on the polished floor; his shadow stretched almost the length of the long hallway. He wandered into Miss Nanney's classroom, and was surprised to find it deserted. Miss Nanney did not live there after all. He walked over to the tall, open windows and stared down the hill at his uncles' houses, at the depot, the store and the gin, the hotel where Whitey Whiteside stayed. He felt full and content and sleepy; he felt a little sad, but not in an unpleasant way. As long as the sun stayed warm, the breeze soft and pleasant, the sky blue, he would have been content to stand at the window and stare down the hill and think about nothing in particular.

He heard a step at the door and turned to see Penn Carson and Penn's father come into the room. Radford Carson was significantly shorter than the uncles, but more muscular-looking. He was shiny bald on top, but wore a thick, black beard that hung down to the middle of his chest. He wore a crisp, white shirt and a bright red tie. In his hand he carried a fancy felt hat. Aside from his beard, he didn't look like a mountain man; instead he looked like someone smart enough to marry Penn's missionary, schoolteacher mother.

"Daddy," Penn said, "that's Jim Glass." Penn said it in a way that made Jim think they had talked about him before.

Mr. Carson crossed the classroom with confident, almost swaggering strides, staring down at Jim out of black eyes that Jim would have found scary had he not detected the trace of a smile hidden within the fierce beard.

"Jim Glass," Mr. Carson said. "I knew your daddy."

Jim's heart beat faster. "You knew my daddy?"

"He was a friend of mine. We grew up together. We hunted and fished and swam and ran through the woods together, getting into boy-devilment."

Jim stepped closer to Mr. Carson without realizing it. He had heard every story his mother and uncles had to tell about his father so many times that over the years his father had become less vivid. It was as if each story was a favorite shirt that had been worn and washed and hung in the sun so often that its fabric, while soft and smooth and comfortable, was faded to where its color was only a shadow of what it had once been. But because Mr. Carson knew stories that Jim hadn't heard, Jim's father suddenly seemed close by, the way he did sometimes, as if he had left the room moments before Jim got there.

"And I know your granddaddy, too," Mr. Carson said. "Although, if what I hear is right, he ain't long for this earth."

"He's sick?" Jim said.

"Been sick for years, I reckon," Mr. Carson said. "But he's dead old. If he ain't a hundred, he's nigh on top of it."

"Oh," Jim said, because he didn't know what else to say.

Amos Glass had always been the villain in the stories Jim's mother told, but suddenly, without knowing why, Jim didn't want him to die.

"He's a cussed man, Amos Glass," Mr. Carson said. "He was always hard on your daddy, especially once he got out of prison and got back up on the mountain. And he was hard on your granny, too. A lot of folks said she died just to get out of living with him, and I reckon there might be some truth to that."

Jim nodded, less worried now about the sick man up on the mountain and again sorry for the two people he knew best from his mother's stories — his father as a boy, a good, Christian boy, and his father's beautiful, sickly mother, Amanda Gentine Glass, the two of them waiting and praying on the mountain while Amos Glass, released from the federal penitentiary, blew toward them like a bad wind.

"Jim Glass," Mr. Carson said again, still staring at Jim. "You favor your daddy."

"What was my daddy like?" Jim asked.

"Your daddy was a fine feller. Did what he said he was going to do. Stood his ground when he had to. You could trust him."

"Was he a good ballplayer?"

"He was an all right ballplayer, but he didn't have time to play much ball. When Amos was in jail, he had to work all the time to keep him and his mama from starving. Then, when Amos got out of jail, Amos kept him on a pretty short lead."

"Could he fish?"

"Now there," Mr. Carson said. "That's one thing Jim Glass could do. He could fish. And he could hunt. There was times him and his mama didn't have anything to eat except what he could catch and shoot. And something else he could do was shoot. He was as good a shot as I ever saw."

"Tell him about that time y'all went squirrel hunting," Penn said.

Jim stared at Penn in disbelief. Penn knew stories about Jim's father that Jim didn't know.

Mr. Carson hung his hat on the back of a chair and leaned against the windowsill. He tugged at his beard as if pulling on it opened a door that let his thoughts out.

"One time, this was right after ol' Amos had got

out of jail and back up on the mountain, me and
your daddy were out in the woods a-squirrel hunting, and we just happened to come up on the place
where Amos had his still. That was the first thing
Amos did, when he got back from Atlanta, was start
back up making liquor. Me and your daddy, when
we smelled the mash a-cooking and happened to
think where we were, we sneaked through the laurel and looked down and seen ol' Amos down
there working. His still was down in a little creek-
hollow, and he was making a batch. We watched
him for a minute, and the next thing I know, your
daddy says 'watch this,' and brings up his rifle —
we both had .22's — and aims down in the hollow.
I thought he had decided to shoot Amos, and I
can't say that I much blamed him. But what he was
aiming for was the boiler. Your daddy never did
drink none, and he thought it was a sin. He takes
careful aim, and he squeezes one off, and sure
enough, he shoots a hole in the boiler and the
mash starts pissing out on the ground. The next
thing I know, Amos had jerked up *his* rifle — he
had a .30-30 — and started shooting up into the
laurel where we were. Now son, let me tell you
something, we lit out of there. We weren't worried
about him catching us — he was seventy-five or
eighty or more then — but he durn sure could've
killed us.

"After we got away from there where we weren't
worried about him catching us or seeing us, your
daddy said, 'Rad, give me a shell. He's going to
count mine.' And I said, 'Jim, you're crazy. He ain't
going to count your shells.' But he said, 'No I'm

not. The old man's going to count my shells, and if he comes up one shy, he's going to kill me.' So I gave him a shell and we went on home. Sure enough, that night, Amos got a light and came up in the loft where Jim was sleeping and he stuck a pistol right up under Jim's chin and he said, 'Boy, give me your shells,' just like Jim thought he would. Amos knew Jim had a new box of shells, which is fifty, and he knew Jim had brought home four squirrels, and he also knew that Jim was a good shot and didn't waste ammunition. Amos poured those shells out on the bed and he counted 'em and the whole time he kept that pistol right up under your daddy's chin. But when he counted 'em, there were forty-six, just like there was supposed to be, and ol' Amos, he takes his light and his pistol and he goes back down stairs, and he didn't never say anything else about it."

A Victory of Sorts

FROM HIS place in line with the rest of the
fourth graders, Jim could easily see the crisp dollar
bill tacked to the top of the greasy pole. The money
belonged to the boy who could climb high enough
to claim it, a task made almost impossible by the
poplar log's slick sap and smooth wood. A swelling
crowd pressed in close and cheered loudly for each
boy as he struggled to reach the money, but, despite the crowd's encouragement, not one of the
smaller boys, the first and second graders, had
made it more than a foot or two off of the ground.

Jim wanted the dollar, but he wasn't as intent on
winning it as he might have been earlier. Mr. Carson's story still swirled brightly inside his head. He
could see Lynn's Mountain rising in the blue distance above the heads of the crowd. Amos Glass
still lived on the mountain. That simple fact gave
Mr. Carson's story the immediacy of a dream that
for a moment had slid with its strangeness into the
waking world. Jim thought, *My daddy wasn't afraid.*

And he thought, *My daddy outsmarted Amos Glass.* And because Amos Glass still lived in a place Jim could see, it was easy for him to imagine his father up there somewhere, maybe slipping through the woods with a squirrel rifle or fishing in a clear creek. And these thoughts opened up a longing he could feel tingling in the backs of his legs. He wondered if his father, looking down from the mountainside, would be able to see Aliceville — the red school on top of the hill, the crowd gathered on the playground, the boys waiting in line to climb the greasy pole, and the one boy, staring up at the mountain, who wanted to see him more than anything.

Penn, who stood in line in front of Jim, turned around.

"I think one of us is going to get the dollar," he said. "We're the first big boys."

"Looks that way," said Jim. "Have you ever seen my granddaddy?"

Penn nodded. "He used to sit out on the porch before he got sick."

"What does he look like?"

Penn shrugged. "He's real old."

"Did you see him a lot?"

"Some. His house is pretty close to ours."

"You've seen his house?"

"Yep."

In Jim's mind, Amos Glass's house had long been a place where history had happened, like Fort Sumter or Gettysburg.

"That's where my daddy grew up," Jim said. "That's where my daddy lived until he came down here."

"I know."

Penn turned again toward the greasy pole — it was almost his turn to go — but then turned back to Jim.

"Good luck, I guess," he said.

"You too," said Jim.

When Penn's turn came, he took a running start and leapt onto the pole, a tactic that gained him precious altitude. None of the other boys had thought to try it. He began to slide back down instantly. He hugged the pole mightily with his arms and scraped at it with the hard edges of his shoe soles. Sliding still lower, he gritted his teeth and attacked the pole furiously. In rapid succession he pushed with his feet and pulled with his arms and pushed with his feet and pulled with his arms, until — everybody saw it — he checked his descent and for a few precious seconds actually began to inch upward. The crowd let out a hoarse shout.

Over the roar, Jim could hear Mr. Carson yelling, "Come on, *Penn!* Come on, *Penn!*"

Penn fought back to the height at which he had leapt onto the pole and then moved slightly past it, kicking and slapping at the pole, his feet then his arms gaining traction for a fraction of a second and then slipping. His face slowly turned scarlet and took on a furious, almost frightening expression; Jim could tell that Penn had simply decided he was not going to touch the ground until the dollar was his.

But after a while, despite Penn's determination, his energy began to flag and his effort slowed. He lost a little of the height he had gained, redoubled his effort, gained it back, then lost a little more. Even as he slid lower and lower on the pole, the fierce look on his face did not change. Jim could see that he wasn't going to give up. Eventually, however, even though he pulled his knees almost into his chest, his feet were just a few inches off of the ground. Even then, with his last remaining energy, Penn fought the greasy pole. Jim found himself almost pulling for his rival.

When Penn's feet touched the ground, he collapsed onto his back and lay on the ground with his eyes closed. His hair was wet with sweat and his breath came in ragged gasps. The insides of his forearms were red and raw-looking, and the front of his overalls was shiny and tacky with tree sap. Mr. Carson came out of the crowd and helped Penn to his feet. As he led Penn away, the crowd clapped respectfully.

"Good try, Penn," Jim said as Penn walked by.

Penn nodded but did not look up.

The crowd grew silent for a moment, but when Uncle Coran bellowed, "Go get 'em, Jim!" everyone began yelling his name.

Jim looked at the pole, which suddenly seemed as tall and forbidding as Jack's bean stalk. He felt his heart flutter coldly inside his chest, a small shirt frozen on a clothesline, the winter wind blowing through it. He knew suddenly he couldn't climb the pole, but did not know how to get out of trying. He heard Uncle Zeno's voice separate itself from the noise and urge him on: "Let's go, Doc. You can do it!" He felt weak and dizzy, but his feet began to inch toward the pole, without his willing them to. Suddenly, the thing that had been holding him back snapped inside his chest, and he ran forward in a rush, as if preparing to jump out of a hayloft or from a tall rock into the river.

He leapt onto the pole as Penn had done, bruising both shins and almost knocking the wind out of himself. He immediately felt himself sliding toward the ground. He squeezed the pole as hard as he could with his arms and scrabbled at it with his feet and pushed into it with the heels of his shoes. He felt himself stop sliding. He put his weight on both feet and pushed himself up. He was surprised when he was able to stand up almost straight before his feet slipped. He squeezed the pole tightly against his chest and pulled his legs up underneath him. When he pushed with his legs, he again traveled up the pole. The pole was still slippery, and climbing it wasn't easy, but Jim suddenly knew that it was something he could do.

In short order he passed the height Penn had reached, and kept going. The pole was more slippery higher up, but it was also skinnier, allowing him to wrap his legs around twice, which kept him from sliding downward. Because the pole was slippery, he could only move up a few inches at a time with each push of his legs, but he also made steady progress. Jim looked up and saw the dollar bill getting closer and closer. He looked down and saw the ground a surprising distance below him. His heart leapt because he knew he was going to be the winner.

Finally, he reached up and almost delicately

plucked the dollar from the tack that held it to the pole. He shoved it into the pocket of his overalls. He hooked his arm over the top of the pole and looked down into the crowd beneath him, trying to find Mama or the uncles. His name rose up to him in a shout, but as he scanned the faces shouting up at him, he didn't see anyone he knew. Uncle Zeno would say later that Jim had looked like a possum, grinning from a tree limb. And Jim would say, much, much later, that, with half the county baying around the bottom of the pole, he had felt like one.

The only person Jim recognized from the top of the pole was Penn. And he was surprised to see that Penn was smiling and clapping, as if he was pleased that Jim, and not himself, had made it to the top of the pole and claimed the prize. Penn waved at Jim, and for a heartbeat Jim felt bad about winning the money. He slid down the pole with his prize in his pocket, where he found Mama and the uncles waiting for him. The uncles clapped him on the back so hard it almost hurt.

"Oh, Jim," Mama said, "your daddy would be so proud of you."

Uncle Al scooped him up and sat him on his shoulder. Wherever he looked people were smiling up at him and clapping. He felt like the king of the world. He patted his pocket to make sure that his dollar was still there.

Jim walked backward down the hill, holding his dollar over his head with both hands, so Mama and the uncles could see it better.

"Pretty proud of yourself, aren't you boy?" Uncle Coran said.

Jim sang, "I got a dollar. I got a dollar."

"All right, Doc," Uncle Zeno said. The uncles didn't like bragging.

Jim kept singing. "I beat Penn Carson. I beat Penn Carson."

"Jim . . . ," warned Mama.

"Well, I did," Jim said. "I beat that hillbilly."

"Jim!" Mama said.

She and the uncles stopped and looked at Jim sadly. Uncle Zeno lowered himself to one knee and said, "Come here, Doc."

Jim lowered his arms and pushed the dollar back into his pocket. He walked forward until Uncle Zeno clasped him by the shoulders and looked him in the eye.

"That's right," Uncle Zeno said. "You beat Penn Carson. But do you know why?"

Jim shook his head.

"You beat him because he had most of the sap from that poplar tree on the front of his overalls. That made the pole not as slippery for you. You won because he helped you."

"Nobody ever gets anything all by himself," Uncle Al said.

"It's the truth," said Uncle Coran.

"Think of where we would be if it wasn't for the uncles," said Mama. "We wouldn't have a thing in this world."

"Do you understand?" Uncle Zeno asked.

Jim nodded.

Uncle Zeno turned him around and lightly swatted him on the bottom.

"Let's go on home then."

And when Jim started again down the hill, part of him was ashamed of his bragging, and ashamed of the resentment he harbored toward Penn, a boy of whom, he now admitted to himself, he was jealous. But in another part of him, the memory of beating Penn was too fresh. Every time he thought of looking down from the top of the pole while the crowd yelled his name, his blood raced anew in memory of his triumph. The two parts of him argued between themselves as he walked down the hill. One side wanted to be a boy the uncles would approve of; the other side silently sang, *I got a dollar. I got a dollar.*

King

FIRST JIM and Uncle Zeno passed Abraham's ancient truck clacking up the state highway toward New Carpenter. Abraham waved out the window as they sped by. Then they passed the convicts: two lean white men burned the color of dirt by the sun, their shirts tied around their heads like turbans, digging beside the highway with long post-hole diggers. The convicts were chained together at the ankle, but Jim didn't see that until the last moment before the truck passed, when, just as he noticed the chain, one of the convicts glanced up and for a long heartbeat looked him in the eye. As Jim wheeled in the seat and watched the two convicts, and the sleepy-looking guard who watched over them, grow smaller in the rear glass, he felt deliciously frightened. He worried for a moment that the convicts, who, with each hole they dug, got closer to Aliceville, were chained only to each other, and not to anything else.

Beyond the convicts, they passed the conical,

evenly spaced piles of earth that marked the holes the convicts had dug. Each hole would eventually hold a tall, black pole; each pole would hold up the wires that brought electricity to Aliceville. The convicts, whom Uncle Zeno had nicknamed Coran and Al, had been digging the holes all summer, although as of yet, not one of the holes had sprouted a pole.

The day was a Saturday, an Indian summer day so bright and warm that it made Jim want to roll around in the grass and stretch like a cat. He and Uncle Zeno were on their way to New Carpenter with the windows rolled down. The trees on the far sides of the fields were gold and yellow and orange, which became — when Jim squinted enough — a fire on a western prairie. Uncle Zeno, as usual, had to see a man about a dog. Jim told Uncle Zeno he would help him put the dog in the truck.

Three miles outside of New Carpenter they topped a slight rise in the road and saw in the distance, for the first time, a long line of black power poles tottering toward them like giants, the cross pieces that would support the stretched wires sticking out to the sides of each pole like short, stiff arms.

"Well, well, well," said Uncle Zeno. "Looky coming here."

He slowed down and pulled off the highway up next to the dirt pile marking the last empty hole before the lines of poles began. He and Jim got out and walked to the front of the truck to take a look. The poles seemed alive to Jim, vaguely ominous in their great, skinny height, standing still only because he was watching them. He found that by moving his head a little to one side, he could make all the poles disappear behind the nearest one; that by leaning far to one side, and then quickly to the other, he could make the whole line wag like a tail. He stopped when he heard Abraham's truck approaching behind them on the highway. He didn't want Abraham to see him acting like a kid. Abraham pulled up even with Uncle Zeno and stopped without pulling off the road.

"Mr. McBride?" he yelled over the racketing of his truck. "Did y'all break down? Do you need any help?"

"No thanks, Abe," Uncle Zeno yelled back, pointing at the power poles. "We're just looking."

Abraham nodded and waved and drove away. He had two bushels of apples in the back of his truck. Jim felt a little irritated that Abraham would be in New Carpenter while he and Uncle Zeno were. He still secretly resented Abraham for taking the good hoe on his birthday.

"I guess they'll put a pole in this one next week," Uncle Zeno said, nudging the piece of scrap board covering the hole with his toe. "Let's see if the jailbirds are doing a good job."

He leaned over and flipped the board off the hole. The hole was so deep and shadowed that it took a moment for Jim's eyes to adjust enough to see the bottom.

"This is a good hole," Uncle Zeno pronounced. "It's the same size at the bottom that it is at the top.

A lazy man digs postholes that are big at the top and little at the bottom. You can't set a post in a hole like that."

Jim studied the hole more closely, and made a point of trying to remember what Uncle Zeno had said. Jim made a point of trying to remember everything the uncles said about work.

"It looks to be eight or nine feet deep," Uncle Zeno said, glancing over at Jim. "You want to find out how deep it is?"

Jim nodded and looked around for something to stick down in the hole. Then he noticed that the hole was big enough for his shoulders to fit through, and realized what Uncle Zeno had meant. Uncle Zeno got down on one knee and took Jim by the wrist. Jim stepped off into the hole and Uncle Zeno lowered him into the ground.

"Don't drop me," Jim said, looking up at Uncle Zeno just before he passed out of the sunlight on his way down.

"Hang on, Doc," said Uncle Zeno.

Inside the hole, the air was immediately cool, November-feeling. The ground smelled old, forgotten, and made Jim think of crickets singing late in the evening before the first frost. When Uncle Zeno lay flat on his stomach, Jim still hadn't found the bottom of the hole. He bicycled with his feet, trying to find solid earth; he tried looking down but could not see past his legs into the darkness. When he looked up, he found Uncle Zeno's body blocking most of the daylight. He squeezed Uncle Zeno's wrist tighter.

"I ain't touched the bottom yet," Jim said. "You can pull me up now."

"My hand's slipping, Doc," Uncle Zeno said in a strained voice.

"Don't drop me," said Jim.

"I can't hold on," said Uncle Zeno.

"*Please* don't drop me," Jim said. He scrabbled at the sides of the hole with his feet, trying to climb out.

When Uncle Zeno let go, Jim thought he was going to fall a long way, but his feet hit the ground after only a few inches. He found himself crouched in the bottom of the hole, his heart racing, both of his arms held over his head, his mouth open to yell — a position that made him feel a little silly once he realized he wasn't falling. He lowered his arms to his side and slowly realized there was no reason to be afraid. The hole had more room than he had thought. He turned completely around in one direction, and then back the other way.

"What are you doing down there, Doc?" Uncle Zeno said from up above. Jim could tell that Uncle Zeno had dropped him on purpose.

"Nothing," said Jim, looking up. Uncle Zeno's face was dark, but his head was surrounded by a halo of blue light.

"What am I going to tell your Mama?"

"Tell her you put me down in a hole," Jim said.

Uncle Zeno didn't say anything for a moment. "We better not tell her that," he said quietly.

Something in Uncle Zeno's voice made Jim imagine his father sitting in the bottom of a hole much like this one. He imagined that his father was neither happy nor sad, just sitting there, waiting for something. It wasn't necessarily a *bad* feeling; the hole wasn't really an unpleasant place to be. It was just lonesome. Directly in front of his eyes, a rock stuck out of the dirt wall of the hole. He poked at the rock with a finger, thinking, *I'm the only person who has ever seen this rock. I'm the only person who will ever see this rock.*

"We better get you out of there, Doc," Uncle Zeno said, lowering his arm into the hole.

Jim studied Uncle Zeno's big hand dangling above him. When he jumped, Uncle Zeno firmly grabbed his wrist. He pulled Jim quickly into the bright daylight and set him on his feet beside the hole. The familiar world temporarily seemed strange to Jim, bright, more beautiful than he remembered. He was glad to be back.

Uncle Zeno made a big fuss brushing the dirt off of Jim's overalls.

Jim was sorry he had made Uncle Zeno feel bad. "That was pretty funny," he said.

"Humph," said Uncle Zeno. "Your mama probably wouldn't like knowing I dropped you down in a hole, would she?"

"No," Jim agreed. "She probably wouldn't."

Not long after they got back on the road, they passed the sign marking the town limits of New Carpenter. Jim never tired of the moment when the state highway rolled in from the countryside and twisted down a little hill and changed itself into Main Street. Seeing the town all at once on a

Saturday was like suddenly seeing the ocean: it made Jim breathe a little faster until he got used to it. Brick buildings leaned in on both sides of the street. Whole flocks of people scurried in and out of the stores and among the growling traffic. Down on Trade Street, farmers from all over the county parked their trucks shoulder to shoulder in a line four blocks long and hawked vegetables and apples and watermelons and roasting ears of corn. Sharps and would-be sharps wandered up and down among the farmers hoping to trade guns or knives or sell poor-looking dogs. At the far end of town, Trade and Main, city and country, collided and crossed in a honking, scary intersection, above which the tall white courthouse rose importantly from a large green lawn. On the lawn beneath the trees, tough-looking, young mill hands with the afternoon free gathered in their Saturday clothes. They laughed and argued and looked at people and occasionally fought. The whole thing was watched over by a gruff old policeman named Hague who carried a blackjack and blew his whistle and yelled at kids when they jaywalked. Aliceville always seemed a little quiet to Jim, almost like church, after he visited New Carpenter. As far as Jim was concerned, the uncles didn't bring him here nearly often enough.

Uncle Zeno parked the truck on Trade Street and turned to Jim. He said, "You think you're old enough to keep an eye on that courthouse clock and be back here by one?"

Jim nodded rapidly. The uncles had never turned him loose in New Carpenter before.

"All right, then," said Uncle Zeno. He removed a dime from the bib pocket of his overalls and gave it to Jim. "You stay out of trouble, now, and don't tell your Mama I let you go off by yourself."

"Yes, sir!" Jim said.

Once Jim reached Main Street, his excitement at being there alone quickly chilled. Everywhere he wanted to go, he found groups of kids, New Carpenter kids, all strangers, already in possession of the place. Kids swarmed like flies around the drugstore counter, where Jim had wanted to get some ice cream; four tough-looking boys were squatted down in the hardware store beside the display case holding knives; a covey of girls giggled into the dime store just as Jim got there. Soon he began to feel that all the other kids in town were watching him, that they felt sorry for him because he didn't have any friends. He grew angry at all the kids in New Carpenter for just being there, and angry at himself because he was not brave enough to go where they were and tell them who he was.

Jim was wandering toward the courthouse when Penn Carson yelled his name from the other side of the street. Jim was glad to see someone he knew. He waved his arm back and forth over his head as if signaling a locomotive in a train yard. He looked up and down Main Street, but did not see a hole in the traffic that would let him cross.

Penn pointed toward the courthouse, and they walked toward the intersection, Jim on one side of the street, Penn on the other. At the intersection, Penn waited for the light to change and ran across Main Street toward Jim.

"Hey, Jim!" Penn said, as if they were the oldest friends. "Do you want to go exploring?"

"Yeah!" Jim said, his appreciation of New Carpenter returning in a rush.

He followed Penn across Trade Street and up the stairs leading to the courthouse lawn. A smoking gauntlet of mill hands lined the sidewalk that crossed the wide yard. Mama said that mill hands carried switchblade knives and got drunk and cut each other. Jim didn't dare look at them.

At the base of the courthouse steps, Penn stopped and looked around furtively, as if they were being followed. "Come on," he said. "I know a secret passageway." He walked to the right side of the steps, motioned for Jim to follow him, and ducked behind the wall of fat boxwoods that ringed the courthouse. Between the courthouse and the boxwoods was a space just wide enough for the boys to pass through single file. They hurried along the front of the building, invisible behind the thick bushes. After they turned the corner, Penn stopped Jim and pointed down at a man's footprint, its heel mark deep and distinct in the soft ground.

"Convicts!" Jim whispered. "We saw them on the way here. I bet one of them escaped!"

"That's what I was thinking," said Penn.

"There's not enough sign to track him."

"He might be down there," Penn said, pointing at a stairway leading into the basement of the courthouse.

"He might be," Jim said. "Have you ever been down there?"

"No," said Penn, "but I'll go if you will."

"You think we'll get in trouble?"

"I hope not."

They crept to the stairwell, crawled underneath the handrail, and dropped down in front of the basement door. They crouched to stay out of sight.

"See if it's locked," Penn said.

Cool, ammonia-smelling air rushed out around Jim when he opened the door. Ahead of him lay a dark hallway divided across the middle by a thin band of barred sunlight.

"Look," Jim whispered. "A jail cell!"

"I don't know," said Penn. "Do you think we should look inside it?"

"I will if you will," Jim said.

They crept down the hallway, their backs flat against the wall, almost to the boundary of sunlight on the floor. Jim was afraid to go any farther. He stared down at the shadow of the bars, at the dust motes suspended above the floor. He was about to tell Penn they should go back when Penn shoved him into the light. Through the cell door Jim saw a mill hand sitting on a bench beneath a barred window. He raised his head and looked at Jim with a sad, bruised face. One of his eyes was swollen almost shut. His lower lip was split, and the front of his white shirt was splattered with blood. Jim could not move away from the door, nor take his eyes off of the man. He stared at him the way he might stare at a strange, growling dog blocking his path. One corner of the man's mouth twisted up in a crooked smile.

"Boo!" he said, lunging suddenly toward the door.

Jim stumbled backward, where Penn grabbed him by the arm.

"Run, Jim!" he yelled.

They ran down the hall, out the door, up the stairs, and across the lawn through the mill hands. They ran across Trade Street without waiting for the light. They did not stop running until they were halfway down Main Street, where they slowed to a jog, then to a breathless walk, their hands on their hips as they tried to breathe. When they finally plopped down on the bench outside the barbershop, Jim could feel his hands shaking, but he wasn't afraid anymore — just excited. Strangely, he felt like laughing.

Penn started to grin. "You should have seen your face," he panted.

"At least I didn't yell," said Jim.

When they started laughing, it took them a long time to stop. Then they leaned back against the bench and sat for several minutes without talking. Jim turned his face up to the sun. He felt absolutely content.

"I'm glad," Penn said finally, "that the mountain boys . . ."

"And the town boys," Jim cut in.

". . . aren't here."

"Me too," said Jim. "They would mess everything up."

It was Jim's turn to choose a place to explore. He led Penn to the alley between a ladies' store and a

lawyer's office. The alley ran all the way to the un-
named street that paralleled Main. Jim stopped a
few feet into the alley and pointed at the brick wall,
where someone had drawn a skull and crossbones
in chalk. Underneath the skull and crossbones was
written the word "KING."

"Who do you think King is?" Penn whispered.

Jim frowned. "He couldn't be a pirate," he said.
"It takes forever to get to the ocean from here."

"Then why the skull and crossbones?" asked
Penn.

"Maybe he's a murderer," Jim said.

They walked slowly toward the sunlit space Jim
could see at the end of the alley. Every few steps
they encountered fresh warnings, each more fierce
than the one that preceded it: "NO TRESPASSING
KING;" "BEWARE KING;" "IF YOU GO PASS
HERE YOU WILL DIE KING." Jim had always
wanted to explore this alley, but now he wasn't so
sure. His feet felt too heavy to move. The alley had
grown darker and colder, as if it were a canyon between two tall cliffs. He would have run all the way
back to Main Street, but he didn't want Penn to
think he was afraid.

Penn picked up a small, white rock and drew a
circle around the word "PASS."

"At least he spelled his name right," he whispered.

Jim put his hand over his mouth to keep from
giggling out loud.

They tiptoed out into a small courtyard that
opened onto the narrow, muddy street. The

ground was littered with cigarette butts and broken bottles. On the other side of the street was the back of an unpainted shack almost overrun with blackberry briars. An enormous crown was chalked onto the wall. Underneath the crown was written "YOU DIE KING."

"I don't know, Jim," Penn said. "What if King really is a murderer? What if he's not playing?"

Jim considered the possibility. "Let's get out of here," he said.

When Jim and Penn turned to go back the way they had come, they saw two older boys running toward them down the alley. Another two boys ran into the courtyard from the small street. They quickly found themselves surrounded. The boys wore dungarees, not overalls. They closed in around Jim and Penn until Jim could smell their hair oil, the cigarette smoke on their clothes. Jim guessed they were New Carpenter boys, mill-hill boys, seventh, maybe eighth graders. There was no way to get away from them. Jim wanted to tell Penn that if he didn't fight, these boys would kill them.

Almost as if reading Jim's mind, Penn whispered, "I'm with you, Jim."

Jim felt a little better, but not much. He picked out the least scary-looking pair for when the fight came, but the idea of fighting the bigger boys — and of what they would do to him and Penn — made him feel sick inside.

One boy was obviously the leader. He was stocky, bordering on fat, but his arms were almost man-sized. He wore a felt cap shaped like a crown. He stepped up so close to Jim and Penn that he was almost touching them. He had tiny black eyes set above big round cheeks.

"I'm King," he said, pointing toward the alley. "Can't you hicks read?"

"Better than you can spell," Jim said.

King shoved Jim hard against the wall. "Did I say you could talk, hick-boy?"

Penn pushed King. "You leave him alone!" he said.

"That was the biggest mistake you ever made," King said, pushing up his sleeves.

Over King's shoulder Jim saw Abraham walk into the alley. Abraham didn't look at Jim.

"Hey, old man," said King. "No 'coons allowed back here."

Abraham's eyebrows went up briefly and he reached into the pocket of his overalls. Jim heard a click and suddenly there was a knife in Abraham's hand.

"Hey," said King, backing toward the street.

Abraham stepped closer, his face a blank.

All four of the boys took another slow, backward step.

"Hey," King said again.

"Hey," said Abraham.

The boys turned and broke for the street. Jim could hear their feet splashing in the mud as they ran away.

Abraham still didn't look at Jim. He stared at the street where the boys had gone. He reached into his other pocket and pulled out an apple.

"Hey, Abraham," said Jim.

"Sit down, Mr. Glass," Abraham said. "Against that wall right there."

Jim backed up and sat down against the wall.

"Who's that?" Abraham said, indicating Penn with the knife.

"He's my friend," Jim said. "Penn Carson."

"Sit down, Mr. Carson."

Penn obediently sat down beside Jim.

"Slide over," Abraham said, indicating with the knife that he wanted them to sit apart. He walked over to the wall, turned, and sat down heavily between Jim and Penn. Jim and Penn stared at the knife. With great formality Abraham began peeling the apple. Jim noticed that this hands were shaking.

"Abraham?" Jim said.

"Them boys was following you all over town. I followed them boys. They ain't good boys."

"I know," Jim said.

"What are you doing back in this alley?"

"We were just playing," said Jim.

"Well, you ain't playing no more."

Jim stared at the apple as Abraham peeled it, at the peeling snaking toward the ground. Even though his hands were shaking, Abraham managed to keep the peeling in one piece.

"Oh, Lord," Abraham mumbled. "Yea, though I walk through the valley of the shadow of death, I will fear no evil."

Jim suddenly felt as if he were going to cry.

"What's going to happen to us?" he said.

"Just hush," said Abraham.

Jim heard people coming down the alley.

"All right now," said Abraham. "If I say go, you go. Mr. Carson, you find the policeman. Jim, you find your uncle."

Jim and Penn started to stand up.

"Not yet," Abraham said. "We're going to eat this apple here."

Hague the policeman stepped into the courtyard, followed by King. Hague carried a blackjack. Abraham reached up and took off his hat.

"That's him!" King yelled, looking out from behind the policeman. "That's the nigger tried to cut me!"

Abraham cut a slice from the apple and handed it to Jim. Jim took it and ate it. Abraham cut another slice and handed it to Penn.

Hague stared at them a long moment.

"Thy rod and thy staff," Abraham whispered.

Hague turned and looked at King. "Nobody here tried to cut you," he said.

"He did, too!" King whined. "He did try to cut me!"

"You're crazy," Jim said. "That's the craziest thing I ever heard. He was just peeling an apple."

King squinted his eyes at Jim in a threat.

"What an imagination," said Penn.

"I will dwell in the house of the Lord forever," whispered Abraham.

Hague pointed across the street.

"You the punk been writing all this garbage on the walls?" he said.

"What?" said King, his mouth and eyes widening. "What?"

"Get out of here," said Hague.

"But . . . ," King said.

Hague tapped King on the backs of his legs with the blackjack. King jumped each time as if the blackjack were hot.

"I said take off," said Hague.

King pointed at Jim. "I won't forget who you are," he said.

"That's a dumb hat," Jim said.

Abraham handed Jim another slice of apple. Jim chewed it slowly while staring at King.

"Don't make me tell you again," Hague said, tapping King's legs again with the blackjack.

King stared around wildly and disappeared up the alley. The policeman stared up the alley until Jim could no longer hear King's footsteps.

Hague turned to Abraham and pointed the blackjack at him. "Don't you *ever* do that again. You understand me?"

Abraham bowed his head and nodded.

Hague pointed the blackjack at Jim and then at Penn.

"And you boys," he said, "might ought to go find your daddies."

"Yes, sir," said Penn.

Jim thought about telling Hague that he didn't have a daddy, but thought better of it.

"Now," Hague said. "I'm going to take a walk down to Trade Street. And the three of you might want to follow me."

"Yes, sir," Jim said.

"Yes, sir," said Penn.

"Thank you, sir," said Abraham.

Hague led the way up the alley. Jim and Penn followed him closely. Abraham brought up the rear four or five steps farther back. When they reached the street, Jim saw King and his friends watching from a safe distance away. Jim stuck his tongue out at them, knowing that whenever he came to New Carpenter in the future, he would have to stay close to the uncles.

When the four of them reached Depot Street, Jim saw that Mr. Carson had miraculously parked next to Uncle Zeno. Penn reached over and lightly punched Jim on the arm. Jim punched his friend back. Behind them Abraham began to hum.

Blackbirds

*T*HE BLACKBIRDS *come out of the northwest in a great, raucous, glittering stream. When the birds at the front of the flock begin to drop in a hooking curve and light in the walnut tree at the edge of the field, the rear of the flock looks as if it is only then crossing the dark hump of the mountain. Cissy has never seen anything like it; her face turned upward, she stares into the twilight until the last bird has passed overhead.*

The flock transforms the tree into a picture of its lush, summer self — only, instead of leaves, its limbs have sprouted birds. She realizes it is a thing she misses already, the fullness of a tree, and is thankful for the illusion. The day has been neither warm nor cold, fall nor winter; the weather lacked anything she could feel. It seems to Cissy that the din raised by the roosting birds is the only sound she has heard all day.

The boy runs up breathless beside her.

"Mama, how many birds do you guess that is?" he asks.

"I don't know. Hundreds. Thousands. A multitude. I don't know."

She sees him start to count, then abandon the idea as hopeless.

"If Uncle Zeno shot up in there with his shotgun, how many birds do you think he would kill?"

Cissy looks down at the boy, then back at the tree. It trembles in the failing light.

"Jimmy," she says. "Why would you ask me something like that? Why would you want Zeno to shoot those birds?"

"I bet he could kill a hundred," says the boy. "Maybe two hundred."

Cissy's eyes begin to fill. She doesn't know if the boy can even hear her; she doesn't know if she has spoken out loud. She blinks so that she can see clearly.

"What's wrong, Mama?" he asks.

Cissy waves him away, doesn't dare look at him. She unties her apron and takes it off. She pushes her hair behind her ears. She takes a few hesitant steps toward the tree, then breaks into a run; she reaches down with one hand and pulls up her skirt so that she can run faster; she is surprised by how good running feels.

The boy trots along beside her, his eyes wide. He has never seen her run before. She has not run a step in his lifetime.

"Mama," he says. "Mama, where are you going?"

Cissy begins to wave the apron over her head.

"Shoo!" she yells. "Fly away! Leave!"

When she closes to within thirty yards of the tree, the flock lifts as one body with a percussive, ripping sound, as if the air itself is tearing. It moves away from the tree, a creature with a single mind; it flattens and stretches *out and winds fluidly across the field, like water seeking a low place.*

Cissy runs a few more steps, still flapping the apron, then slows to a stop. Her heart throbs wildly inside her chest; her breath burns in her throat. She stares at the gaunt limbs of the walnut tree, the empty sky. She hears the birds shouting in the dark woods along the river. They sound angry, indignant, accusing. In the morning they would be gone. She wheels and stares down at the boy. He backs up a step. When she steps toward him, he backs up again. She points at the tree.

"There, Mr. Glass," she says. "It's winter now."

BOOK IV

Cold Nights

December 12, 1934

Dear Mr. Whiteside,

I am informed by my brothers that by my refusal to re-marry, I am somehow depriving my son Jim of the masculine companionship necessary for the proper forming of young boys. Which perplexes me. I ask you, Mr. Whiteside, how can it be that my son suffers from a lack of male companionship and Love, when each of my brothers would gladly lay down his life in order that Jim might live? What can four men possibly provide for a young boy without a father that three cannot? And were I to marry a man who desired to take Jim and me away from this place, away from his beloved uncles, would Jim then not suffer because one man occupies the space formerly occupied by three? If Jim is to be so immeasurably helped by addition, could he not also be equally harmed by subtraction?

But still, despite my protests, I am told by my brothers that you wish to speak to me formally and make your suit. (Which surprises me somewhat — can it truly be said that we even know each other, Mr. Whiteside? You are a man I recognize as someone with whom my brothers do business, nothing more — and what can I be to you other than a woman, a widow, you have seen sitting on a porch, or perhaps walking to church with her son and brothers?) You should be flattered, Mr. Whiteside, that my brothers have chosen to champion you, for they are fine, honest, Christian men and good into their meddling bones. I am sure that in everything they do and say and suggest they have my best interest, and that of my son, in their hearts and seek only to honor me in their endeavors. Which is the only reason I am writing you today, Mr. Whiteside. They tell me that agreeing to see you is in my best interest and, more importantly, in the best interest of my son Jim. You must understand that I live only for Jim, who walks through my small life, in the footsteps of his father who died just over ten years ago, and brings me joy. Because my brothers — whom I love and honor — suggest that I would be acting in a manner that would bring harm to Jim if I do not see you, I will see you. I will hear what you have to say.

But I must warn you, Mr. Whiteside, I cannot imagine what you might say to me that would make me change my mind. I do not expect you to understand what I am about to say, but the simple truth with which I live every day is that I am a married woman. (Do you not think me insane for saying such a thing?) When I took Jim Glass for my husband, I forsook the possibility that I would ever take another man for my husband. Believe me, Mr. Whiteside, no one understands better than I that my husband is dead. He died alone in a field while hoeing cotton in the sun one week before Jim was born. These are the unadorned facts of my life. But so is this — even though my husband is dead, Mr. Whiteside, I still feel married. How could I possibly take another husband?

Yet my brothers, knowing that I feel this way, have encouraged you. They are wise men, and good, and are perhaps working for Our Lord in ways not yet made manifest by Him. (Although I pray without ceasing and doubt in my deepest heart that this is so!) So I will see you. I will see you once and hear what you have to say. Do not get your hopes up, Mr. Whiteside. I am doing this only because my brothers say it is what I should do, that it is the best thing for Jim, for whom I thank God *every day. So I will see you. The next time your travels as a salesman bring you this way, speak to one of my brothers, who will make arrangements, as this is their idea and responsibility, and therefore only fitting.*

I am, with all honesty,

Sincerely yours,
Elizabeth McBride Glass

Christmas Eve

*J*IM WOKE with a start when someone placed a rough hand over his mouth. Above him loomed a dark figure. "Doc," whispered the figure, "don't be afraid."

It was Uncle Zeno. Jim felt the fright that had bloomed inside his chest folding back into itself and growing smaller.

"Do you promise to be quiet?"

Jim nodded.

"Do you promise you won't say a word until we get outside?"

Jim nodded again.

"Good," Uncle Zeno whispered. He removed his hand from Jim's mouth. "Get dressed. We've got places to go."

When Jim threw off the covers, the cold in the unheated room rushed at him and peeled away whatever warmth was still left from the quilts. He hurriedly put on his socks, his shirt and overalls, then his shoes.

He didn't really think about where they were going, or think about how strange it was that they would go anywhere during the middle of the night on Christmas Eve. He was simply excited. Uncle Zeno had come for him; it didn't matter where they were going.

After Jim buttoned his coat, Uncle Zeno pointed at the window, which, Jim noticed for the first time, stood wide open. Jim walked around the bed to the window and looked outside. Uncle Coran and Uncle Al stared up at him from the yard.

"We're waiting for Jim Glass," Uncle Coran whispered.

"I'm Jim Glass," Jim whispered back.

"Oh," said Uncle Coran. "You better jump out the window, then."

Jim swung his legs over the windowsill and pushed himself into Uncle Coran's arms. Uncle Coran took a stumbling step backward and fell down, still holding Jim. Embarrassed, Jim scrambled to his feet. Uncle Al clapped his hand over his mouth and pointed at Uncle Coran. Uncle Coran lay on the ground and silently shook with laughter.

"Shh," Uncle Zeno hissed from the window. "Daggummit. You're going to wake up Cissy."

Uncle Zeno stuck one long leg out the window, then the other, and lowered himself backward, holding on to the sill with his arms. He looked back over his shoulder and tried to see the ground. Finally, he let go and clumped noisily into the yard.

"I can see the star," Uncle Coran said from the ground, pointing.

Jim looked up, but saw thousands of stars, the

dusty, bright streak of the Milky Way wiped across the sky. He didn't know which star Uncle Coran was talking about.

"O Little Star of Bethlehem," Uncle Coran sang softly.

"*Town*," Uncle Al whispered.

"O Little Town of Bethlehem," sang Uncle Coran.

Uncle Zeno and Uncle Al grabbed Uncle Coran's hands and pulled him to his feet.

"You're going to get all of us skinned alive," Uncle Zeno said.

The uncles stood and grinned at Jim.

"What's wrong with y'all?" asked Jim.

Uncle Coran looked offended. "It's Christmas," he said.

"We've got a surprise for you," said Uncle Zeno.

"Yep," said Uncle Al. "A surprise."

The uncles led Jim around the house and onto the state highway. They stopped in the middle of the road and turned to face the uncles' three houses.

Jim looked nervously up and down the highway.

"We're in the road," he said.

"There ain't nothing coming," Uncle Zeno said. "It's the middle of the night."

"Above thy deep and dreamless sleep, the silent stars go by," sang Uncle Coran.

"You're flat," said Uncle Al. Uncle Al prided himself on his pitch.

"I am not," Uncle Coran said. "You're just listening flat."

"Are y'all drunk?" asked Jim.

"What?" said Uncle Zeno. "We're not drunk, are we boys?"

"We're not drunk," said Uncle Al.

"Not by a long shot," said Uncle Coran.

"They why are y'all acting so funny?"

"We're not acting funny," Uncle Coran said. "You're just looking at us funny."

"We just want you to see something," said Uncle Zeno.

"In the middle of the road?" Jim asked.

"It's as good a place as any," Uncle Al said.

Jim looked up and down the highway again, then up the hill at the school. He looked at the uncles' dark houses, at the store, the cotton gin, the depot, and the hotel. There was nothing to see. Everything was dark and peaceful and starlit and cold.

"What is it?" Jim asked. "What do you want me to look at?"

"You'll see in just a minute," Uncle Zeno said. "Just wait."

Uncle Al held both arms out to the dark world. "Let there be light," he said.

"Allie," chided Uncle Zeno.

Again Uncle Al threw his arms out wide. "Let there be light," he said, louder.

"Don't be blasphemous," Uncle Zeno said.

"Why is that blasphemous?"

"Because God is the one who said, 'Let there be light,' and this is Christmas Eve."

"I know what day it is," Uncle Al said. "And there

ought to be one day a year when I can say whatever it is I want to say without somebody telling me I ought not to say it."

"Was Jesus born tonight or tomorrow night?" Uncle Coran asked.

"Tonight," said Uncle Zeno.

Uncle Coran scratched his head. "Then that would make today Christmas Day, not tomorrow."

"What?" said Uncle Zeno.

"Think about it," said Uncle Coran. "If Jesus was born before midnight tonight, then that would make all day today Christmas Day and yesterday Christmas Eve. But if he was born after midnight, then that would make Christmas Day tomorrow like it's supposed to be, and this Christmas Eve."

"I don't know what you're talking about," Uncle Zeno said. "How can yesterday be Christmas Eve when today is Christmas Eve? Everybody knows when Christmas Eve is."

"Doggone it, Zee," Uncle Coran said. "You ain't listening to me. I bet Jim understands. You understand what I'm talking about, don't you, Jim?"

"No, sir," said Jim.

"Then you weren't listening, either."

Now Jim felt offended.

"I'm cold," he said.

"Let there be light," said Uncle Al.

At that moment, miles away in New Carpenter, a man looked at his watch and threw a switch. Electricity blinked through the wires to Aliceville.

And the lights in the uncles' houses came on.

Jim thought for a heartbeat that the uncles' houses had exploded into flames, and involuntarily took a step backward. His mouth dropped open.

Uncle Coran let out a long, low whistle. "Do something else, Allie," he said.

Uncle Al stared at his hands.

"I better not," he said.

"Look," Jim said, as soon as he was able to speak.

"We thank thee for thy miracles," mumbled Uncle Zeno.

All three of the uncles briefly looked at the ground.

"Those are the biggest houses I ever saw," said Uncle Coran. "I never knew we lived in such big houses."

The uncles' houses indeed suddenly seemed magnificent. Jim shivered as he stared at them. Every window blared with fierce yellow light, except for Mama's, which was dark.

"Why don't we wake up Mama?" Jim asked.

"Your Mama needs her rest, Doc," Uncle Zeno said.

"And she wouldn't like it out here in the cold no way," said Uncle Al. "She'd make us all go inside."

"Oh," said Jim.

"Look," Uncle Coran said. "Look up there."

On top of the hill the new school had transformed into a castle filled with light. The ground was lit up all around it.

Jim and the uncles walked up the hill. The bright light streaming out of the empty school made it seem even larger and more imposing than it did during the day. Jim reached out instinctively and hooked his fingers through the hammer loop on the leg of Uncle Zeno's overalls.

When they reached the school yard, they walked up close to the building, but stopped short of touching it. Uncle Zeno pulled his watch from his pocket and studied it.

"Look at this," he said. "It's ten after twelve, and I can see what time it is."

Uncle Coran and Uncle Al and Jim leaned toward Uncle Zeno and looked at Uncle Zeno's watch.

"Well, I'll be," said Uncle Coran. "It's ten after twelve."

Jim climbed up on the steps and looked down into Aliceville as if he were a prince and the town was his kingdom. Soon he felt weighted by a prince's worries. The brightness of the few lights burning in Aliceville only magnified the darkness that still surrounded the town. The uncles' electric lights drew fragile boundaries around their houses; around those boundaries a blackness crept that suddenly seemed as big and powerful as God. Jim had never noticed the darkness before. He felt on the verge of knowing something that he didn't want to know. He jumped off of the steps to be closer to the uncles.

Uncle Zeno dropped a heavy hand onto Jim's shoulder.

"Home looks different now, huh, Doc?" he said.

Jim forced himself to keep smiling; he willed his eyes to stay wide. He didn't want to disappoint the uncles.

"Yes, sir," he said. "It sure does."

On the way home the uncles did not seem as merry. Nobody talked as they headed down the hill. Suddenly the night seemed even colder. Jim felt as if they were marching into a strange town — a kind of town different than the one he had always known. Such a town would require a different kind of boy to live in it — a boy smarter and stronger and braver than Jim knew he was. He didn't know how to live in such a place. The world had changed in an instant, but he was still the same. He looked at Mama's dark window and shivered. When he looked up at the stars, they did not seem as bright.

My dearest, dearest Husband,

*If you are looking down on me — as I have believed
for the last ten years, as I must believe if I am to continue to rise each morning and live without you — what
must you think of me? If you are looking down on me
from your high place and know my thoughts and my
heart, you already know that I have agreed to see another man and consider his suit. Did this break your
heart and make you turn your back on me? Or do you
really wish — as I have heard over and over until I am
sick of hearing it — that I should marry another?
Would it really please you — as everyone says — if I
"got on with my life?" Is it possible that you could really
look down on me from heaven and watch me speak to
another man in the ways of women and men and not
feel pain?*

*My brothers tell me that I am hurting Jim, our son, by
not taking a new husband to be his father. And I cannot
countenance the idea of hurting Jim any more than I
can entertain the idea of causing you even another moment's pain, which leaves me torn and bewildered. If I
do not marry again, I harm your son; if I do marry, I
harm you. What my brothers do not understand is that
even though you died, I swore in my heart that it did not
matter, that we were still married, that your death was
only a momentary separation. I told myself that you had
gone away to prepare a home in a better place and that
you would send for me when it was ready. I swore that
this was how I would live my life, that I would be faith-
ful to you and married to you until such time we could
be reunited. This was my secret oath. And now I have be-*

trayed that oath. Does this not make me the vilest kind of low woman? Did Jesus not tell us that the thought of sin is as bad as the sin itself? How can you possibly forgive me for what I have done?

I know that God left me on this earth to insure that our son grow up to be the kind of man you would have raised him to be, and therefore see that your death was not in vain, but what do I do when my brothers tell me that God's will is different than I perceive it to be? Does God speak to them and not to me? Am I really as alone as I feel in my heart? By insisting that I speak to this man, my brothers force me to act in a manner I find despicable. I want to shout out at them, I AM A MARRIED WOMAN! Can they not honor my marriage? Can I not choose to be married to you even if you are dead? Is this not my sacred right?

I just don't know what

At the Tenant House

A FTER SUPPER, Mama told Jim he could go sit with the uncles in the store. Jim leapt up from the table. The store was where the uncles retreated evenings when they wanted to be by themselves. Most of the time they didn't let Jim go with them.

The moon shone brightly on the snow. Jim watched his shadow slide thinly in front of him as he crunched down Depot Street. The snow had been on the ground almost a week; it lay frozen and pitted and muddy where people had walked or driven, but the moonlight made it look fresh and new. The uncles said that when snow stayed around for more than a few days it was waiting for its mate. Jim hoped that it would snow again soon. The frigid air made his chest burn pleasantly; he tried to feel warmth on his face as he passed through the clouds made by his breath.

At the store, Jim crouched and sneaked toward the window. He crept through the white square the electric light drew on the snow. He rose up slowly and peeked inside. Uncle Zeno and Uncle Coran hunkered over a game of checkers. Uncle Al stood above them and studied the board with a frown. Nobody moved and nobody spoke. Jim decided that he would rather stay outside.

He headed toward the hotel, thinking that maybe he would throw a snowball at Whitey Whiteside's window. Whitey was passing through town on his regular run. Jim had no idea what he would say if he got Whitey to come outside, and tried without much luck to think of something. As he approached the hotel, the front door swung open and Whitey stepped onto the porch. Jim froze where he stood. Whitey wore a suit — but no overcoat — and one of his snappy hats. He held on to a porch post and leaned out and looked up at the moon; he removed his watch from his vest pocket and tilted it toward the light. When he walked down into the yard and started toward the fields, Jim decided to follow him.

Whitey walked out of town and turned onto the faint track that led through the woods to the tenant house where Mama had lived with Jim's daddy. Jim, who had been following about fifty yards back, stopped at the edge of the woods and wondered what Whitey was doing. The track led solely to the tenant house. Beyond the tenant house lay only open fields, and, across the fields, the river. Mama, of course, spoke of the tenant house as if it were a site in the Holy Land, but nobody else spoke of it at all. Why would Whitey go there?

As Jim stepped off of the road, he noticed another set of footprints leading into the woods. These prints were smaller than the ones made by Whitey's big shoes. Jim began to feel a little scared. Who did the other set of footprints belong to? What if Whitey was up to no good? What if he was a bank robber meeting his gang at the empty house? Jim cautiously entered the woods, careful to avoid the open track. He didn't want anyone to see his footprints later. Whitey was out of sight somewhere ahead. Every few steps Jim stopped and listened and peered through the trees. The limbs of small trees reached out and scratched at him as he passed, and the leaves frozen beneath the snow crackled underneath his feet.

He reached the edge of the clearing where the tenant house sat just as Whitey stepped onto the porch. Small cedar trees poked up through the snow. Beyond the old house, the smooth, white fields glowed peacefully. Whitey knocked on the door. When the door creaked open on its rusty hinges, Jim knew, without knowing how he knew, that Mama was inside. Mama had made the other set of footprints in the snow. Mama was waiting in the tenant house for Whitey.

Jim understood that he was witnessing a transaction so important and secret that he was not supposed to see it. Once he had peeked through Mama's keyhole and watched her bathe — an act that made him so ashamed he could not look her in the eye for days. That's how he felt now, only he could not make himself stop watching. He squatted and sat motionless in the woods and tried to breathe quietly, like a rabbit waiting for a hunter to pass.

Whitey stepped forward, but stopped without passing through the doorway. His voice reached Jim as a low mumble without discernible words. He held out his arms as if puzzled or imploring, and asked what Jim recognized as a question. Jim didn't hear Mama reply, but what she said made Whitey turn away from the door and step to the edge of the porch, facing away from the house.

With his back to the door, Whitey talked to Mama a long time. He gestured with his hands and stopped occasionally to listen. Once he looked up at the sky and shook his head. Finally he raised both hands as if asking Mama to be quiet. He removed a white handkerchief from the breast pocket of his suit, shook it open, and spread it onto the porch floor. He knelt, still facing away from the door, placing his right knee on the handkerchief. Jim's breath turned jagged in his throat. A sweat bloomed all over his body, even though he had been cold the moment before.

Whitey was proposing to Mama.

Mama spoke sharply from inside the house — Jim heard her for the first time — and Whitey stood up quickly. He took his hat off and put it back on. He reached into his jacket pocket and removed something small. Still facing away from the door he extended his arm behind him and implored Mama to take it. Jim held his breath, waiting to see if Mama would step forward.

But Mama stayed inside the tenant house.

Whitey's arm eventually sank to his side as if he had been holding up a great weight. Without speaking again, he stepped off of the porch and walked across the clearing and up the track into the woods.

After Whitey had gone away, Jim stood still and waited for Mama to come out of the house. When she finally appeared, Jim's heart pounded as if she were a deer or a spirit. She carefully closed the door, turned, and looked down at the handkerchief Whitey had left on the porch. She picked it up, held it briefly to her nose, and put it into her coat pocket.

Mama had walked only a few steps into the clearing when her legs collapsed as if something heavy had fallen on top of her. She sat down in the snow and raised her hands to her face. Jim felt two warm tears roll down his cheeks. He held his arms toward Mama and squeezed his hands open and shut as if trying to pull her toward him, but he was afraid to leave his hiding place in the woods.

Mama finally dried her eyes on her coat sleeve and climbed to her feet. She squeezed her coat closed at the neck and trudged across the clearing toward the path home. At the edge of the woods, she turned and looked back toward the tenant house. Jim heard her say his name, but knew she wasn't talking to him.

BOOK V

Quiet Days

A Game of Catch

THE LAST week of March, a slow, cold rain fell until water stood ankle-deep on the playground. Each day that week was wetter than the day before, and it seemed to Jim that only the trees and the buildings kept the low sky from dragging on the ground like a sheet. The roads grew so muddy that the bus from Lynn's Mountain could not make it to Aliceville. School seemed empty without Penn and the mountain boys there. Although it was time for baseball season, Jim didn't even bother taking his glove when he climbed the hill to school.

Nor did the rain let up the first week in April. Every morning Uncle Zeno stepped onto the back porch, looked up at the sky, and shook his head. The river reddened and swelled and climbed toward the tops of its banks. On the days the rain fell hardest, it lapped out into the lowest bottoms, where it curled in slow, searching eddies over the unfamiliar ground. On the days the rain slackened, it slid back out of the fields, leaving behind slicks of trash and wide, shallow lakes that from a distance looked very deep.

Mama and the uncles grew cross with the weather and then with each other. Uncle Al could not get into the fields to begin the spring planting. He sat around the house and the store and glowered. One day he got so mad that he went back to his house and slept all afternoon. The mules, fat from a long winter of corn and rest, stood sopping and still in the muck of the barn lot, their ears flat, their heads down as if ashamed.

Uncle Zeno could not run the gristmill because the high creek would flood the mill house if he opened the race. He brought the emery wheel into the kitchen and ground knives and axes until they were sharp enough to shave the hair off of his arm. Mama complained about the uncles being underfoot and tracking mud into the house. She complained about the noise Uncle Zeno made with the emery wheel; she said she would rather have dull knives than listen to it. She said it was good weather for catching a sickness, and felt Jim's forehead with her palm almost every time he came into the room, which made Jim cross, too.

Only Uncle Coran did not seem to mind the rain. When bad weather drove the farmers out of the fields, it inevitably herded them into the store. After dinner on most rainy days, the store filled up with farmers who loafed around most of the afternoon, waiting for the clouds to break and the fields to dry, drinking Coca-Colas and smoking until a great blue cloud hovered just beneath the roof.

The days Uncle Coran hated most were the ones where everybody was out in the fields working and he sat for hours around the cotton gin and the store without anyone to talk to. Unlike everyone else, Uncle Coran seemed to get happier and happier the longer the rain fell.

Finally, on the second Saturday in April, a hazy, tentative sun, the color of an old quarter, appeared behind the thinning clouds. The store was busy that morning, but emptied quickly when the sky began to brighten. After dinner Jim sat with the uncles in the empty store, where the uncles talked about President Roosevelt until Jim began to fall asleep. Roosevelt was an interesting subject only when the odd Republican happened by. Jim wandered outside without any real destination, where he threw rocks into mud holes, but without any real pleasure. Everywhere he stepped the ground sucked at his shoes.

Around two o'clock he began to listen for the Carolina Moon. The Carolina Moon was so sleek and modern that it seemed to come from some beautiful future Jim longed to see. It blasted through Aliceville without noticeably slowing. Its only acknowledgment that the town even existed was a single admonishing shout of its whistle at the crossing. Jim listened for the train, but all he could hear in the distance was the river racing smoothly through the woods, back inside its banks now, but still full and high.

When the train finally approached, Jim could tell by the sound that it was going to stop in town.

He ran up onto the porch of the store and stuck his head inside the door. The uncles looked up. "The Carolina Moon is stopping," Jim said. The uncles stared at Jim for a moment and then stood as a group, almost as if he were a minister and had asked them to sing a hymn.

Jim got to the track just in time to see the great, gleaming locomotive, streamlined and fast-looking like a bullet, its steam engine breathing mightily, edge past the station and stop. The last of its silver passenger cars rolled to a standstill abreast of the station. Pete walked out onto the platform, looked at Jim, and motioned importantly with the flat part of his hand for Jim to stand back. Up the track two men in overalls climbed down out of the cab and crawled underneath the locomotive. One of the men carried a toolbox.

The uncles walked up beside Jim. Their reflections were distorted in the shiny sides of the passenger car. They had short, stumpy bodies and long, pointed heads, which made Jim smile. The windows reflected only the sky above Aliceville, which kept him from seeing inside the train. Ragged scraps of cloud slid from window to window to window, moving toward the front of the train as if looking for seats.

"Hey, Pete," Uncle Zeno said. "What's wrong with the Moon?"

"Ran over a cow," Pete said. "Get a good look at her. She ain't going to be here long."

"I heard she can run seventy-five miles an hour," said Uncle Coran. "How fast can she run, Pete?"

"I don't know for sure," Pete said. "Fast enough

to get you there and back before you know you're gone, I guess."

"Right," said Uncle Coran. "Seventy-five miles an hour."

A door opened near the rear of the car, and a black-suited conductor with a thick gold watch chain stretched across his vest grabbed onto the handrail and swung himself down to the ground. Without looking at Pete or the uncles or Jim, he started for the head of the train, walking uneasily on the sloping gravel of the roadbed to avoid the soggy ground. A mud hole filled with red water stood in the low place just off the grade. When the conductor got to the locomotive, he leaned over and looked in between two of the wheels.

"That's the head man right there," said Uncle Zeno.

Jim heard somebody sneaking up behind him and turned to see Penn. Penn's eyes were bright, and his face was shining and red, as if he had been running. Jim grabbed Penn's hand and pumped it hard. Penn hadn't been to school in over a week.

"Hey, Penn," Jim said, maybe a little louder than he meant to.

"Hey, Jim" said Penn. "And Mr. McBride and Mr. McBride and Mr. McBride." Unlike Jim, Penn never forgot to be polite.

"Penn," said Uncle Al.

"Howdy," said Uncle Coran.

"Mr. Carson," said Uncle Zeno, looking down at Penn's legs, which were caked in thick mud up to his waist. "How're you today?"

"Pretty good," said Penn. "I'm kind of tired,

though. Daddy and I got stuck in the mud coming down here, and I had to get out and push. My britches are so stiff I can hardly walk."

"Guess what?" Jim said. "The Moon ran over a cow."

"Why didn't the cow jump over it?" Penn said.

He laughed and whacked Jim on the arm. Jim whacked him back. They stood and rubbed their arms and grinned at each other.

"It's been too wet to play ball," Jim said. "With y'all stuck up on the mountain we wouldn't have had enough to play a game anyway."

"Sorry about that," Penn said. "Maybe the road will dry out and we can get a game in this week."

Down at the far end of the train the conductor stood up and started back toward the station. When he drew abreast of Jim and Penn, he stopped and looked at them and motioned for them to come closer.

"I need to speak to you gentlemen," he said.

Jim pointed at his chest. "Us?"

"You," said the conductor.

Jim and Penn looked at each other and started slowly forward. They jumped when they got to the mud hole below the grade. Penn didn't quite clear it and came down in the edge of the water with a splash. They walked hesitantly toward the conductor, who looked very important. As the conductor of the Carolina Moon, he was easily the most important person Jim had ever been around. He had white hair and a fine, merry face. He motioned the boys closer, leaned over, and put his hands on his knees. He looked soberly into Jim's face and then into Penn's. Jim thought maybe they had done something wrong, but couldn't figure out what it could be.

"Guess who's sitting in that car right behind me?" the conductor said.

"Who?" said Jim and Penn.

The conductor leaned closer and whispered, "Ty Cobb."

Jim's mouth dropped open. Penn squinted and rubbed his forehead as if he hadn't understood what he had heard.

"The Georgia Peach," said the conductor. "I thought you boys might like to know."

"Boy, did we ever!" Penn said, extending his hand. "Thank you."

"Thank that heifer we ran over," said the conductor, shaking Penn's hand. Then he shook Jim's hand, too.

He drew a gold watch big as a clock out of his vest pocket and studied it. He looked at Jim and Penn and winked. "Late, late, late," he said. He tucked the watch back into his pocket. He grabbed hold of the rail beside the high steps and lightly swung himself up. He held on to the rail, leaned out away from the car, and looked toward the head of the train.

Jim jumped over the mud hole and ran over to the uncles. Mr. Carson had joined them. Penn hesitated at the mud hole, jumped, and missed clearing it again.

"What did he say, Jim?" asked Uncle Al.

Jim opened his mouth but found that he could not speak. He closed his eyes and gulped a mouthful of air. He could hear somebody yelling inside his head, Ty Cobb! Ty Cobb! Ty Cobb!

Penn shoved Jim impatiently. "*JIM*," he said.

"Ty Cobb," Jim said. "He said Ty Cobb is on the train!"

The uncles' heads jerked up as if pulled by invisible strings. Ty Cobb, because he was from Georgia, had always been one of the uncles' favorite players.

"Ty *Cobb?*" said Uncle Zeno.

"In that car right there," Penn said, pointing.

Uncle Al whistled. "Boy," he said. "Boy."

"Ty Cobb, huh?" said Uncle Coran. He winked at Jim and Penn and tilted his head toward the station. "Ty Cobb was the best ballplayer there ever was," he said loudly.

"Humph," said Pete from the platform. "Babe Ruth is the best ballplayer there ever was." Pete was from Ohio. He was a big Yankees fan, the only one in Aliceville, so far as Jim knew.

"Babe Ruth was born in Baltimore, you know," Uncle Coran said.

"So?" asked Pete. "What does that prove?"

"Well, Maryland is below the Mason-Dixon line," Uncle Coran said.

"And Maryland was a slave state," added Uncle Al.

Pete looked disgusted. "You're trying to tell me that Babe Ruth is a *southerner?*" he said.

"Shoot, you ought to be able to tell that by the way he can hit," said Uncle Zeno.

The uncles started to grin. Even Mr. Carson smiled behind his black beard.

"All right," Pete said. "I can see which way this train's headed. And this is where I'm going to get off."

Uncle Coran winked again.

"Ty Cobb," said Uncle Zeno. He looked at the conductor and stepped forward, stopping at the edge of the mud hole. "Excuse me, sir," he said. "I understand that Ty Cobb is on this train."

"Yes, sir, he is," said the conductor.

"Where's he headed?"

"We're taking him to Atlanta," the conductor said. "After that I couldn't tell you."

"Could you tell these boys here what Mr. Cobb is like?"

The conductor looked at Jim and Penn and considered a minute.

"Mr. Cobb," he said carefully, "is a paying passenger."

"Hmm," Uncle Zeno said slowly. He took off his hat and scratched his head. "By any chance could these two boys here get on the train for just a minute and maybe meet Mr. Cobb?"

"Oh, please," said Jim.

"Please, please, please," said Penn.

"I'm sorry, boys," said the conductor. "I can't allow that."

"Just for a minute?" Jim said.

"Only paying passengers are allowed on the train."

"Well, all right," said Uncle Zeno, nodding. "We understand. That makes sense. How about if you were to ask Mr. Cobb for an autograph for these two boys?"

The conductor bit his lower lip and then shook his head again.

"Mr. Cobb strikes me as the kind of gentleman who would prefer not to be disturbed," he said. "I think it would be best if we didn't disturb him."

"I'm not surprised," Pete said from the platform. "I'm telling you, Cobb was *dirty*."

"I wouldn't say that too loudly if I were you," said the conductor.

Jim stared up at the train, at the clouds moving across the windows. He could not believe he was so close to Ty Cobb. Ty Cobb was only ten yards away from where he stood. Jim felt his insides quiver; he felt his heart thump. He looked anxiously toward the head of the train. He knew that when the men crawled out from underneath the locomotive, the Carolina Moon would leave and take Ty Cobb with it. It would never stop in Aliceville again. Already Jim could feel how empty the town would be.

Uncle Zeno suddenly clapped his hands together.

"I know what," he said. "Jim, run get your ball and glove."

Jim took off for the house, running as hard as he could. Mud and water flew up around his feet with each step. He ran down Depot Street, crossed Uncle Zeno's backyard, leapt onto the porch, and barged into the kitchen.

Mama was sitting at the table. "Jim!" she said. "Your feet!"

Jim crashed into his room without stopping and dove under the bed. "Sorry," he called out, unwrapping his glove from the oiled cloth in which he kept it. The ball was nestled snugly in the pocket. He put the glove on and ran back through the kitchen. "Ty Cobb is on the Moon!" he yelled.

Mama said, "What?"

Jim jumped off of the porch into the yard. He yelled over his shoulder, "Uncle Zeno told me to get my ball and glove!" By the time Mama got to the door, he was already flying down Depot Street.

When Jim got back to the station, he shoved his ball and glove toward Uncle Zeno. Uncle Zeno pushed them back toward Jim.

"No," he said. "You and Penn play ball right there beside the train. Go on. Let Ty Cobb see how good you are."

"Come on, Penn," said Jim.

Jim jumped over the mud hole. Penn waded through it. In the narrow strip of ground between the mud hole and the road bed, Jim backed a few steps toward the head of the train; Penn backed toward the rear. Jim's first throw almost flew over Penn's head, but Penn reached up and caught it.

"Settle down," said Uncle Zeno.

"Take your time," said Uncle Coran.

Penn's throw came back straight and true. It slapped soundly into the pocket of Jim's glove.

"Atta boy," said Mr. Carson. "Air it out, Penn."

"Easy windup now, Jim," said Uncle Al. "Nice and easy."

Jim felt as if he were pitching in the World Series. He tossed the ball carefully back to Penn. All three of the uncles clapped.

"There you go, Jim," said Uncle Zeno.

Again Penn's throw came back straight and

hard. He had a strange, almost desperate look on his face.

"Jim," he said. "Let me use the glove."

"No," Jim said, this time throwing a little harder. Penn's throw back came so hard it made Jim's palm sting when he caught it.

"Jim," Penn said. "*Please* let me use the glove."

"*No*, Penn. It's my glove."

"Throw him a curveball," Pete said. "Throw him a curveball, Jim."

"I don't know *how* to throw a curveball," Jim said.

"*I* should get to use the glove," Penn said. "I'm a better ballplayer than you are."

Penn was throwing the ball so hard that Jim was afraid he was going to miss it in front of Ty Cobb.

"You are not," he said.

"You know I am, Jim. You know I'm better than you are. Give me the glove."

"You are not better than me," Jim said. He threw the ball almost as hard as he could at Penn. He saw Penn wince when it hit his hands.

"Easy boys," said Uncle Zeno.

"Penn," Mr. Carson said gruffly.

"Jim won't let me use the glove."

"It's his glove," said Mr. Carson.

"But Ty Cobb," Penn said. "Ty Cobb is watching us and I don't have a glove."

"Stop begging, Penn," Mr. Carson said.

"Let Penn use the glove a time or two," Uncle Coran said.

"It's *my* glove," Jim said.

Jim was about to fire one at Penn when he saw

that Penn wasn't looking; Penn was staring beyond Jim toward the head of the train. Jim turned around. The two men who had crawled underneath the locomotive were crawling out. One of the men stood up with the toolbox; the other pushed something long and straight in front of him as he crawled from under the engine. When he stood up, Jim saw that it was a cow's leg, cut off just below the shoulder. The hair on Jim's neck stiffened when he saw it.

"There's the problem," said the conductor.

The man waved the cow's leg over his head with both hands as if it were a flag or a torch. He tossed it into the mud hole beside the track and climbed onto the locomotive. The conductor waved back.

"All a-BOARD," yelled the conductor.

"JIM!" Penn said angrily. "Let me use the glove NOW!"

"I told you NO!" said Jim.

Penn screamed, "GIVE ME THE GLOVE, YOU BABY!"

"Penn!" Mr. Carson said. "You come here to me."

"Game's over, boys," said Uncle Zeno.

The conductor ducked inside the car and closed the door. Jim was furious that Penn had called him a baby in front of the uncles and the conductor.

"BABY!" he yelled. "I am not a BABY!"

He closed his eyes and threw the ball at Penn as hard as he could. It sailed over Penn's head. When it finally hit the ground, it skipped several times over the wet ground and rolled down the grade into the mud hole.

Penn stared at Jim with such hatred that Jim

thought he was going to charge. Jim tensed to fight him. Instead Penn turned to go after the ball. He took a single step and fell face-first onto the ground. Jim heard him say, "Uh-oh." Penn pushed himself up with his hands, but fell again when he tried to stand. He rolled onto his side and looked down at his legs, his face filled with a kind of wonder. The uncles and Mr. Carson ran toward him. Pete jumped down off of the platform. The train lurched and clanked and began to move. Penn lay back and wailed, a forlorn, animal sound that opened up a hole deep inside Jim. When Jim closed his eyes he could feel himself falling and falling.

An Afternoon in the Sun

*P*ENN HAD polio.

The sheriff drove out from New Carpenter and nailed up quarantine notices. The local still stopped at the depot to deliver and take on mail, but nobody got on the train and few people got off. School was turned out and locked up for the summer, even though it was only April.

Jim sat in his room and waited to die. He had squatted on the ground and held Penn's hand. Penn had stared at his legs as if snakes were crawling on them. Now, Jim could feel things crawling on his fingers, and up and down his arm. Mama came in regularly and rested her palm on his forehead to see if the fever had come.

Despite the quarantine, the weather was warm and bright. The breeze blowing up out of the south smelled like the river, and like the earth waking up. The uncles would soon return to the fields. Mama would cook for them and clean their houses. Jim closed his eyes. Everything would go on without him.

Mr. Carson had scooped Penn off the ground and run to his truck. In his haste, he took Penn all the way back up the mountain over the muddy roads, instead of to the hospital in New Carpenter. The uncles wondered if Mr. Carson had simply forgotten about the hospital, or if he only trusted the doctor who lived on the mountain.

Jim sat on a kitchen chair pulled up to the window, his arms propped on the sill. There wasn't much to look at outside. Nobody walked up or down the street or drove into the store yard or stomped in and out of the hotel or the depot. Still, waiting to die was surprisingly interesting. A bird flashing across the sky became an event, a thing to remember; Jim watched three dogs sleeping in the middle of the street as if he had never seen dogs before. When the dogs stood and walked off in the direction of the store, he wondered how they decided where they wanted to go and when it was time to get up. Every so often he stood and flexed his knees and bounced up and down as if he were getting ready to broad jump.

The only time Jim felt sick was when he thought about Penn. The memory of his selfishness the day Penn fell occasionally washed over him and took his breath away. And then he remembered hitting Penn in the back with the ball; he remembered his glee when he beat Penn in the greasy pole–climbing contest; he remembered every bad thing he had ever said or thought about his friend. He wished more than anything that he had let Penn use his glove. He whispered, "Please, please, please," which was at once a prayer for Penn, and a plea for the bad memories to go away and leave him alone.

When Jim opened his eyes, Abraham stood outside his window.

"Hey, Abe," Jim said, sitting up.

"Hello, Mr. Glass," said Abraham. "I didn't mean to wake you up."

"I wasn't asleep," Jim said. "I was just sitting here."

"I was just passing this way," said Abraham.

Jim wondered why Abraham was walking through the yard, and not on the street, but he didn't say anything.

Abraham smiled for no reason that Jim could see. He stretched and yawned expansively.

"I could use a nap myself," he said. "I ate too much dinner."

"Oh," said Jim.

Abraham reached into the pocket of his jacket and pulled out a small parcel wrapped in grease-stained brown paper.

"That reminds me," he said. "I'm too full to eat this fried apple pie. Do you want it?"

Jim eyed the pie. He hadn't realized it before, but a fried apple pie was exactly what he wanted. But he didn't know what Mama would say about his taking it.

"It'll go to waste," Abraham said. "I'd eat it myself, but I'm full as a tick."

Jim remembered that he was waiting to die, and decided he was entitled to a last fried pie.

"All right," he said. "Just so you won't have to throw it away."

Jim took the package and put it under his bed so he could eat it later.

"Well, I guess I better be getting on back," Abraham said. "It was good to talk to you."

"Thanks for the pie," said Jim.

Abraham nodded and took a step backward, but didn't turn to leave; the skin of his forehead suddenly slid toward his eyes; the weight of it forced his eyebrows downward into a frown that made him look very old.

"You're in God's hands, Mr. Glass," Abraham said. "Even when it don't seem like it."

Jim nodded.

"And Mr. Carson, he's in God's hands, too."

"He's my best friend," Jim said.

"Well, there ain't no better place he could be than in God's hands."

"But he's got polio."

"Shoot," Abraham said. "Polio is a thing of this earth. Things of this earth don't mean nothing to God. You just try to remember that."

"I will," Jim said.

"You're going to be all right," said Abraham.

"Okay," said Jim. "I'll try."

Pete carried something heavy-looking inside a paper sack.

"Hey, Pete," Jim said.

"Jim," said Pete.

Jim didn't know what to say next. His conversations with Pete rarely proceeded beyond Pete's greeting.

Pete handed Jim the sack.

"I was kicking around in the coal pile the other day and I found this," he said. "I don't have any room for it. It's yours if you want it. I've got enough junk as it is."

Inside the sack was a large, flat piece of coal covered with the delicate imprints of leaves. Jim couldn't believe his eyes. It was the fossil Pete kept on his desk at the station. More than once Pete had refused to take money for it.

"Gosh, Pete," Jim said. "Thanks. Why are you giving this to me?"

"I just thought I'd clean up the place. That's all. It was either give it to you or burn it in the stove."

Jim ran his finger over the outlines of the ancient leaves.

"There's forty-one different leaves there," Pete said. "I counted them. If you'll look, you'll see that they look like ferns."

Jim nodded in agreement. In the summertime, the wooded banks of the river were cool and lush with ferns.

"It was loaded onto a train at Bluefield, West Virginia, and dumped off here. It's kind of amazing, when you think about it."

"What is?"

"That we can hold something in our hands that was alive millions of years ago. That it was dug up by some coal miner in West Virginia and wound up here in North Carolina with us looking at it."

Jim held the piece of coal closer to his face and for an instant saw the leaves growing green and bright on a strange riverbank.

"When you think about the sun coming up and going down hundreds of millions of times, it kind of makes what's going on today not seem that important."

"I guess so."

"Sure it does," Pete said. "Think about it."

"Okay," said Jim.

"All right, then. There you go."

Jim didn't know what else to say. What was going on today still seemed to him pretty important. He pretended to study the fossil some more.

"How's your mama?" Pete asked.

"She's fine," said Jim, glancing up to see Pete's face rapidly turning scarlet.

"You tell her I said hello."

"I will."

"I think highly of her."

Jim nodded because he didn't know what to say.

Without looking at Jim, Pete began backing across the yard.

"And I think you're all right, too. But don't spread it around."

"I won't."

"You think about what I said about the fossil," Pete said.

"I will," said Jim.

"What's going on today doesn't matter that much."

"Okay."

"Everything's going to turn out fine."

"Okay."

"So don't worry about it."

"I won't."

"And don't play ball like Cobb. Cobb was dirty."

"Do you really think Ty Cobb was on the Moon?" Jim asked.

"Maybe," Pete said. "But there's not much point in worrying about it, now. Whoever he was, he's gone."

"I guess so."

"Okay. Well, 'bye," said Pete.

"'Bye," said Jim.

"Oh," Whitey said, "I almost forgot. This is for you."

He handed Jim a small piece of lead, grooved on one end, flat and misshapen on the other.

"What is it?" Jim asked.

"It's a Minnie ball from the Civil War," Whitey said. "It came out of my grandpa's leg."

Jim stared in disbelief at the piece of lead in his hand.

"Your grandpa got shot in the leg?"

"Battle of Franklin," said Whitey. "They had to cut his leg off. That flat part there, that's where it hit the bone. Broke it all to pieces."

"They cut off your grandpa's leg?"

"Yep," Whitey said. "He was a farmer before the war. But after they cut his leg off, he started preaching."

"Oh."

"He made a pretty good one-legged preacher, too. He gave me that when I was about your age. And I want you to have it."

"Thank you," Jim said. "I promise not to lose it."

Whitey took off his hat, scratched his head, and put his hat back on.

"Look, Jim," he said. "We might not see each other anymore after this."

"How come?"

"I lost my job," Whitey said. "Business ain't so hot, nobody's buying feed and seed much, so the company laid me off. I won't be running my route anymore, so I won't be coming to Aliceville on the train."

Jim swallowed and nodded.

"I hate it," Whitey said. "I'm just tore up about it, but there ain't anything I can do."

"I bet the uncles would give you a job."

Whitey smiled a little.

"We thought about it, but that probably ain't too good an idea."

Jim remembered the night at the tenant house. Mama had never mentioned it. Jim had never mentioned it to Mama.

"I guess not," he said. "What are you going to do?"

"I don't know," said Whitey. "I might go up north and I might go out west. Wherever somebody needs a salesman, I'll go there."

"That's a good idea," Jim said.

"I just wanted you to know that I've enjoyed being your friend. I think you're a good boy."

Whitey stuck out his hand.

"I might have polio," Jim said.

"I'll take that chance."

Whitey squeezed Jim's hand in both of his.

"Jim Glass," he said, "I wish things could have turned out different."

"I know," said Jim.

Whitey cocked his head and raised an eyebrow.

"I saw you talking to Mama that night in the woods."

"You did, huh?"

"Yes."

"Well. Your mama said she was afraid somebody was going to see us, and I guess she was right."

"Did you try to marry Mama?"

Whitey laughed, a sad-sounding noise that came up out of his belly in a chuff.

"I tried," he said. "But she wouldn't have me."

"I figured," said Jim.

"She said she still loves your daddy."

"He died before I was born."

"I know," Whitey said. "It's a sad thing."

"I guess so."

Whitey tilted his head back and locked his fingers behind his neck.

"But we've all got to get on with things, don't we, Jim?"

"Yes, sir."

"We've got to work hard and keep moving and try to do the right thing."

"Yes, sir."

"You take good care of your mama, okay?"

"I will."

"And don't take any wooden nickels."

Before Jim could say, "I won't," Whitey spun on his heel and started across the yard toward the hotel.

BOOK VI

The View from Up Here

Our Boy

LATE IN the morning on Jim's eleventh birthday, something like a miracle happened: Mama gave him permission to go up the mountain with the uncles. When the time came to leave, she even followed them outside to say good-bye. Uncle Coran and Uncle Al climbed into the bed of the truck and sat down in the straight chairs they had placed against the back of the cab. Mama stepped onto the running board and looked in at Jim and Uncle Zeno. Uncle Zeno pressed the starter and the engine shook itself and growled to life.

"You're welcome to come along, Cissy," Uncle Zeno said over the noise.

Mama shook her head.

"Zeno, you know I can't go up there," she said. "I don't think I could stand it."

Jim tried not to look at Mama and looked down at his baseball glove instead. When he glanced up, she took his face into her hands and peered at him intently.

"Jimmy," she said. "You just have to promise me you'll come back."

Embarrassed, Jim blushed and squirmed and freed himself.

"I'll come back," he mumbled.

Mama smiled and stepped back off of the running board.

"Here we go, Doc," Uncle Zeno said. "You ready?"

"I'm ready."

"Wave at your mama."

"All right."

The power lines along the state highway rose and dipped in rhythmic, swooping loops. Young corn waved from the bottoms along the river. Milk cows grazed in the rich June pastures while new calves butted and tugged at their teats. When Uncle Zeno veered off of the highway onto the Lynn's Mountain road, a cloud of red dust bloomed beneath the truck and floated back the way they had come. They rolled past the turnoff to Uncle Zeno's mill and rattled over Painter Creek on the wooden bridge. Jim had never crossed the bridge before, even though it wasn't far from home; until today he had never had reason to travel through the country on the other side.

They drove through a thicket of scrubby locust trees draped with fragrant honeysuckle, and up a mild grade toward the rounded top of a ridge. When they crested the rise, the road fell away into rolling country. In the near distance Lynn's Mountain rose up, its shoulders turned slightly from the way Jim saw them every day from Aliceville, almost as if it were moving toward them as they moved toward it.

"There she is, Doc," Uncle Zeno said.

"Yes, sir," said Jim.

"That's where Penn lives. That's where your daddy came from."

Jim nodded.

"When he left old Amos's house after his mama's funeral, he walked the whole way to Aliceville. Took him all day."

Jim nodded again.

"You never saw anybody as hungry-looking as he was that first night."

"Did y'all give him something to eat?"

Uncle Zeno snorted. "Did we give him something to eat. He liked to ate us out of house and home, just like you."

The road wandered down into a shallow ravine, into the green shade along Painter Creek. The mountain disappeared until they drove back into the sun.

"Since your daddy came from up there, I guess that makes you half mountain man, doesn't it, Doc?"

"I ain't a mountain man," Jim said.

"I see," said Uncle Zeno.

Jim hadn't meant to speak harshly. He looked at Uncle Zeno and tried to smile, but instead felt his face crumpling into something wrinkled and unrecognizable.

"Everything's going to turn out all right," Uncle Zeno said.

"Do we have to go see my granddaddy?" Jim asked.

"We don't have to, but if we don't, someday you'll wish we had. You'll just have to take my word on that."

Jim stared out the windshield at the mountain turning slowly away from them as the road moved momentarily to the east.

"What do I say to Penn?" he asked.

"He's your friend," Uncle Zeno said. "You'll know what to say when the time comes."

"I hope so," Jim said.

The closer they drew to the mountain, the more uneven the land became. White outcroppings of quartz began to spill from the red banks along the side of the road. The road pitched up and down over short, steep hills, on the sides of which clung upland farms. Corn and sweet potatoes and small, cash patches of tobacco and cotton grew in terraced fields that carefully followed the contours of the hills. On one farm a small, rocky pasture fell almost precipitously away from the barn lot. A single white cow gazed at them peacefully from a serpentine trail that switchbacked through the closely cropped grass. At the next house, an old woman hung out a Saturday wash of overalls and work shirts, printed dresses, and wide, white drawers. A pack of mottled blue and white hounds rolled out from underneath the porch and loped after the truck, baying mournfully.

"Your daddy loved to coon hunt," Uncle Zeno said. "And he didn't like to just sit around the fire and listen to the dogs, either. He liked to get out in the woods and run after them. You could see his lantern bobbing out in the dark, and you could hear him hollering. Me and Corrie and Al, we always sat by the fire and waited for the dogs to tree, because that's what our daddy had always done. But your daddy, he ran with the dogs. He always got to the tree not long after they did."

"So my daddy was a good coon hunter?"

"He was," Uncle Zeno said. "Your daddy was good in the woods, he surely was. Of course, he said coon hunting down where we live was nothing like coon hunting up where he came from. He said up on the mountain you had to watch out for panthers. He said panthers lived all over those ridges back then. That's why they call the creek that comes down off of it Painter Creek."

"Did you ever see a panther?" Jim asked.

"No, I never did. But your daddy said he saw one."

"My daddy saw a panther?"

"That's what he said. A panther or something else."

Jim felt something cold scurry down his backbone.

"What do you mean, 'something else?'"

"Well, your daddy wasn't sure what it was. He said it might have been a panther and it might have been a haint."

"A haint?"

"That's what he said, Doc. A haint. He said he wasn't much older than you are right now, probably twelve or so, when this happened. Amos wasn't back from prison yet, but your daddy was old enough to be out in the woods at night. Anyway, he and one of his Gentine cousins went coon hunting. It was a cloudy night, and still, no moon, but a good night to hunt. Your daddy and this other boy had no sooner got their fire built than the dogs came back. And the dogs all had their tails stuck between their legs. They slunk into the firelight and wouldn't go back out no matter how much your daddy and the Gentine boy got after them. Which was unusual, because there ain't nothing a hound dog likes better than to hunt on a damp, still night.

"Your daddy said that he and his cousin were kicking the dogs, trying to make them go back out, when the panther screamed. It was close by, just outside the firelight. And he said its screaming sounded like a woman. He said he'd never heard anything like it in his life, and never wanted to again."

"What'd they do?"

"Well, the first time it screamed, whatever it was, the Gentine boy accidentally kicked over the lantern and broke it. So they backed up as close to that fire as they could get. Then they saw its green eyes moving around out there in the edge of the dark. One minute they could see them, and the next minute they couldn't, but then there they'd be again, behind them this time, or over there. Now, they weren't carrying a gun because when the dogs treed, they were just going to shake whatever it was out of the tree and catch it and put it in a sack and carry it home. Mountain boys like your daddy ain't scared of nothing, Doc. Except maybe panthers. So there they were. They didn't have a gun and the lantern was broke. They didn't have enough pine knots to keep the fire burning all night, and there was a panther stalking them, just waiting for that fire to die out. And the dogs — and these were dogs that would run a bear to ground — were crawling around their ankles, whimpering, scared to death."

"What did my daddy do then?"

"Well, just as the fire was about to die out, the panther screamed a second time. And it was closer. This time it sounded like it was right there in the light where they were. And then it spoke."

"It spoke?"

"It spoke. It said, in a woman's voice, 'Help me, for I am killed.'"

"What happened?" Jim asked. "What happened then?"

"Well, what do you think happened then, Doc? Them boys sold the farm. Your daddy, his cousin, the dogs, everybody, lit out for home in a pile. Your daddy said they were running through the laurel, the limbs grabbing at them and hitting them in the face, and they were tripping and falling down and getting up and scratching and kicking and climbing all over each other in the dark, trying to get away. And your daddy said they could hear whatever it was chasing them, running through the leaves right behind them, panting. Every twenty steps or so it screamed. And every time it screamed, your daddy said he just knew that whatever it was, panther or haint, was going to light right in the middle of his back, and that would be that, he would never live to see another morning."

"Did it get anybody?"

"No, it didn't. Your daddy said that when they ran out into the clearing at home, whatever it was stopped just in the edge of the woods and wouldn't come any further. And he said that the next night, Robley Gentine rounded up all the men and boys and dogs and guns he could find on that mountain, and they tramped around all over those woods, and the dogs cast around all over where the panther had been, but they never struck up a trail, and nobody never heard it scream again, and nobody ever saw it."

Jim stared up at Uncle Zeno. He tried to laugh, but found that he couldn't make a satisfactory noise.

"Did you make that up?" he asked.

Uncle Zeno shook his head.

"No, Jim, I didn't. Me and Corrie and Al got after your daddy every time he told that story. We tried to get him to come off of it, but he never would. Your daddy swore up and down it was the truth, and he was never one to lie about anything."

"How come you never told me that story before?"

"Your mama said she would skin me alive if I did. She said it was too scary."

Jim didn't say anything.

"And Al, he doesn't like it much, either. At least not much since your daddy died."

"How come?"

Uncle Zeno swallowed.

"Well, you know how Allie is, Doc. He's a little superstitious. The way he's got it figured, something bad was after your daddy up on the mountain that night. And he thinks that whatever it was stayed after him and finally tracked him down and got him that day in the cotton field."

Jim didn't know what he was supposed to say. The world suddenly seemed a fearful place.

"But that's just Allie," Uncle Zeno said. "You know how he is. Everything is a sign and a wonder to Allie."

"Why'd you tell me?"

Uncle Zeno shrugged.

"I guess I just figured that if you were man enough to go up the mountain and face Amos Glass, you were man enough to hear about the night the panther talked."

They were close enough to the mountain now that its green flanks filled the windshield. Jim leaned forward until he could see the ridge line again, the familiar blue sky dropping behind it. The mountain seemed to him a live, sleeping thing, lying on its side in the sun.

They crossed Painter Creek on a narrow bridge and entered a long, green valley that ran parallel to the base of the mountain. The valley was checkered by fields and pastures and farmsteads that stretched away into the distance. The creek ran along one side of the valley, its course marked by a ribbon of alder and bamboo and laurel. On the other side of the valley, the mountain reared up out of the lush, tilled bottoms. Jim had never considered before that it was possible to see the exact place where a valley stopped and a mountain began. He studied the line of trees that marked the place the two came together.

Near the head of the valley, the creek sidled closer and closer to the road before turning sharply toward the mountain; the road doglegged and followed the creek. Ahead of the truck, the road vanished into what appeared to be a vertical wall of trees. Jim leaned forward and twisted his head but could not see the ridge line through the windshield. Uncle Zeno looked at Jim and grinned as they rolled into the shade of the woods.

Much to Jim's surprise, the road curved gracefully into the cool, green forest, and remained level for as far as he could see. The broad trunks of the trees rose like columns from a mossy bed of ferns; they did not sprout limbs until far above the ground. To the left of the road, Painter Creek chattered busily over a bed of small, smooth stones. A blue jay flashed brightly in front of the truck, complaining loudly, and was gone as quickly as he had come.

"Did my daddy walk down this road?" Jim asked.

"This is the only way down this side of the mountain," Uncle Zeno said. "This is the way your daddy went to Aliceville."

The road separated itself from the creek and meandered into the forest, rising only slightly.

"He loved this country," said Uncle Zeno. "I don't think he ever got over having to leave. He only left because he had to."

Jim leaned forward, eager to see sights his father

had seen. He thought, *My daddy walked under these trees.* And he thought, *I bet my daddy sat on that rock and rested.* Each time they rounded a curve, he imagined meeting his young father marching through the woods, his few belongings stuffed into the feed sack slung over his shoulder. Jim Glass, Sr., lived only six years after he made the trip. He died when he was twenty-three years old.

"Do you think it was a haint?" Jim asked. "Do you think something bad was after my daddy?"

Uncle Zeno's lips pursed and his brow furrowed.

"No," he said, finally. "I don't think anything bad was after your daddy. I think your daddy had a bad heart. I think your daddy's heart stopped beating and he died. That's all I think. And that's all I care to think."

The road began to buck and heave; it pitched upward and turned back on itself. The switchbacks rolled at them one after another, each more violent than the one before; the road between the curves climbed at a desperate clip. Uncle Zeno downshifted into the truck's lowest gear. Uncle Coran and Uncle Al slid out of their chairs and sat down in the bed. Jim felt a little sick at his stomach.

The ferns from which the trees grew had been replaced by thick walls of laurel and rhododendron whose dark leaves hissed in echo as the truck passed. Around one curve a tiny creek spilled onto the road; it laughed and disappeared into the laurel on the other side as they splashed through it. After a while Jim began to sense that part of the sky was now below them, although the thick undergrowth kept him from seeing into the distance off the side of the mountain.

"Are we up in the air?" he asked.

"We're getting there," Uncle Zeno said.

Finally they climbed around a last snaking curve and drove out into an alpine valley that lay between the peak of Lynn's Mountain on one side and a low ridge on the other. Painter Creek wound its way between the peak and the ridge, as if running across the face of a mountain was a normal thing for a creek to do. High up above the valley, rhododendron and laurel bloomed against the shining green of the trees. The mountainside and the ridge top were dappled with lavender and white. Uncle Zeno slowed and pointed out a wild cherry tree blooming against the side of the ridge. From down below the outline of the ridge disappeared against the greater shape of the mountain; the valley through which they drove lay hidden from view. On the mountain it was still late spring; back home in Aliceville it was already full summer.

Steep-sided hollows separated by spiny ridges dropped down the mountainside and opened into the valley. Out of each hollow flowed a tiny stream seeking the larger creek; up each hollow ran a narrow dirt track. Jim stared up each track as far as he could see. The first house he spotted was a log cabin whose swept yard was enclosed by a split rail fence. A woman stood in the doorway holding a child. In the field beside the house a tall man cultivated young corn behind a yoke of oxen. Jim leaned out the window and stared backward.

At the head of the valley, beyond the end of the

ridge, a bald opened up on the side of the mountain below the road. Jim leaned over Uncle Zeno to look out at the world, but the road turned away from the sky and climbed again toward the summit before he saw very much.

"Can we stop there on the way home?" he asked.

"We'll see," said Uncle Zeno.

They passed a store, a church, a small post office, and the one-room school the mountain boys had attended before it closed. A mile beyond the school they rounded a curve and came upon a sawmill. Uncle Zeno pulled off the road and stopped. Hardwood logs were piled on one side of the saw shed and freshly cut lumber was stacked on the other. From inside the shed came the roar of an unmuffled gasoline engine and the high keening of a saw blade biting through wood. Mr. Carson stepped out of the shadows and strode toward them across the muddy, rutted yard. He wore dungarees and a faded canvas shirt. The legs of his dungarees disappeared into high, mud-clumped, lace-up lumberjack boots.

"That's Penn's daddy," Jim said.

"This is his sawmill," said Uncle Zeno.

Mr. Carson strode up to the truck, spoke to Uncle Coran and Uncle Al, and looked in Jim's window. Wood chips hung like ornaments in his long, black beard; he smelled of gasoline and sweat and fragrant sap.

"Zeno," he said.

"Radford," said Uncle Zeno.

Mr. Carson grabbed Jim's hand and squeezed it what Jim considered a little too hard.

"Hey, Mr. Carson," Jim said, trying not to wince.

"Thanks for coming to see Penn," said Mr. Carson, staring, with what resembled a scowl, straight into Jim's face.

While Jim stared back in disbelief, tears rose in Mr. Carson's eyes and spilled over. They raced down his cheeks and disappeared into his beard as if something were chasing them. Inside the black beard, his red lower lip began to tremble.

"My boy . . . ," he began. "Penn . . ." He turned and faced away from the truck. ". . . thinks the world of you."

He removed a red bandanna from his back pocket and blew his nose loudly. Jim looked up at Uncle Zeno. Uncle Zeno held a finger to his lips. Mr. Carson turned again toward the truck and shook his head.

"Doggone it," he said. "Ever since Penn got sick, I ain't been worth killing."

"It's a terrible thing, what happened to Penn," Uncle Zeno said.

"It ain't nothing you can fight," said Mr. Carson. "That's what I hate about it. It ain't a thing you can shoot with a gun."

Mr. Carson stepped onto the running board of the truck and rapped the door with a knuckle.

"Dad blame it," he said. "Let's go."

Uncle Zeno pulled out of the mill yard and back onto the road. They passed several log cabins and small frame houses before Uncle Zeno pulled into the yard of a large, two-story log house set well back from the road in a grove of tall poplar trees.

Mr. Carson jumped down from the truck. "I'll tell Penn you're here," he said.

He hurried across the yard and bounded up the steps two at a time. Jim slipped his hand into his baseball glove. He felt terrible and weak in his stomach.

Uncle Coran and Uncle Al climbed down from the back of the truck. Uncle Zeno stepped out of the cab and shut the door. Uncle Al rubbed his behind.

"Boy, Zeno," he said. "Is that the best you can drive?"

"I thought I drove all right for somebody born in the last century."

"You drove all right for somebody who don't know how to drive," Uncle Al said.

Jim dragged himself out of the truck.

Uncle Coran pointed at him. "Who's that?" he asked.

Jim didn't even feel like saying his name.

"Boys," Uncle Zeno said, "what do y'all say we stretch our legs a bit? Let's walk back down the road and have a look at Radford's mill."

Uncle Al rubbed his behind again.

"Beats sitting," he said.

"I wish y'all wouldn't go," Jim said.

"We'll be back before you know it," said Uncle Coran.

"I still don't know what to say," Jim said. "What do I say?"

"You'll know," said Uncle Zeno, turning away with a wave.

*   *   *

Jim sat on the running board and stared forlornly at Penn's house. Although constructed of logs, it was considerably bigger than he had thought it would be. The house was framed by a pair of tall, rock chimneys; a porch whose banisters were made of twisted laurel limbs stretched across the front; above the porch lay six wide windows. Red and yellow flowers bloomed in carefully tended beds beside the porch, and a walkway of large, flat stones led from the porch across the yard.

Jim had never asked Penn what his house looked like, and had imagined a one-room cabin perched in the woods on the steep side of the mountain, the world falling dangerously away from its door. He had always assumed that the house he lived in was bigger and nicer than Penn's, and, during the times Penn had edged him in one competition or another, took secret solace in that assumption. He stood up and looked down the road. The uncles had walked out of sight around the curve. He kicked a rock, walked after it and kicked it again. He wondered if Penn was in the house watching him. He wondered if Penn even wanted to see him. He threw his ball into the air and caught it. He took it out of his glove and studied the red stitching, as if some secret were written there.

The front door opened and a woman Jim took to be Penn's mother walked down the steps and across the yard. She smiled broadly and waved. She wore a sky-blue dress and a white apron. Her copper-colored hair was tied loosely behind her neck. Jim waved back. When she got closer, he saw that, while she wasn't as pretty as Mama, something in her face made her nicer to look at. She was wildly freckled, and her smile, which was a little crooked, made Jim want to smile back. She took his right hand in both of hers and held it while she studied him. Her hands were warm and soft. Jim felt himself blush.

"Jim Glass," she said, in a pleasant, although strange, accent, "I am so pleased to meet you. Penn speaks of you with great fondness."

"Thank you, ma'am," Jim said. "It's nice to meet you, too."

She put an arm around his shoulder and led him across the yard onto the porch. They stepped into a painted hallway that ran the width of the house. Through one door Jim saw a parlor with Sunday furniture and a piano; in the room across the hall he saw a tall bed with a canopy. Halfway between the front and back doors, two framed photographs faced each other from opposite walls. In one picture, Penn and Mrs. Carson stood on the steps of a large, brick building with a bell tower. Penn was wearing a white shirt and a necktie. The building looked familiar.

"Do you know where that is?" Mrs. Carson asked.

"No, ma'am."

"That's Independence Hall in Philadelphia. That's where the Declaration of Independence was signed. We were there last summer."

Jim gaped at the picture and pointed at Penn. "Benjamin Franklin and Thomas Jefferson went up those steps?"

Mrs. Carson smiled. "They did indeed. A long time ago."

"And that's where you're from?"

"It is. I grew up in a house not far from there. I came down here to teach school for a year and met Penn's father."

In the other photograph, Penn and Mr. Carson grinned extravagantly from what seemed to be the edge of the world. Only a metal guardrail separated them from yawning space. Mr. Carson's beard blew out to the side in a stiff wind. Penn nervously glanced toward the chasm. Far below, an immense city stretched away until it disappeared into a gray haze. Jim had never imagined a city could be so big.

"Gosh," he said. "Where's that?"

"New York City. The Empire State Building," said Mrs. Carson. "I wanted Radford and Penn to see Manhattan. I think their mouths hung open the whole time we were there."

Jim looked up at Mrs. Carson and blinked. He wanted to tell her about something important, but couldn't think of anything. He suddenly felt ashamed and small.

"Why do y'all live here?" he asked.

Mrs. Carson looked momentarily puzzled. "Because," she said, "this is our home."

"Oh," said Jim.

He followed her out the back door and onto a covered mud porch. The yard sloped away toward a small creek. Two rocking chairs faced the creek, and Penn sat in one of the chairs. Jim stopped uneasily at the top of the steps.

"Is he okay?" he asked.

Mrs. Carson tilted her head and smiled at Jim as if he were the one she felt sorry for.

"I think he's just fine," she said. "Why don't you go see for yourself? He's been waiting for you."

Jim trudged down the steps and across the yard. He felt mad at the world. He was angry at the uncles for bringing him up here, and mad at Mama for letting him come. He thought about going to wait in the truck for the uncles to come back, but his legs wouldn't stop moving down the slope of the yard. Penn had been to the top of the Empire State Building. Penn had been to Independence Hall. Jim had no idea what to say to a boy who had seen the things Penn had seen. And he had no idea what to say to a boy who had polio. When he walked past the rocking chairs, his stomach dropped as if he had jumped off of something high. He took a deep breath and turned around.

"Hey, Penn," he said.

"Hey, Jim," said Penn.

The two boys stared at each other and grinned, then shook hands awkwardly, as if a grown-up were making them do it. Jim looked down at Penn's legs before he could stop himself. Penn slapped his right leg twice with an open palm.

"It's this one," he said. "I can't move this one."

"Oh," Jim said. "I'm sorry."

Penn shrugged. "It's okay," he said. "It could've been a lot worse." He kicked his left leg straight out. "This one's fine."

"At first, down in town, they said you were going to die."

"That's what they said up here, too."

"Did you think you were going to die?"

"Not really. I don't remember."

Jim rolled a stick back and forth with his toe. "Will you . . . ?"

"Maybe," Penn said.

"Really?"

"The doctor in Winston-Salem says it might come back. You can't ever tell."

"Oh."

"You get used to it, though."

"What does it feel like?"

"Sometimes it hurts. Mostly it just feels asleep."

Penn slapped his leg again and stared at it. Jim stared at it, too.

"Oh, well," Penn said.

"Oh, well," said Jim.

"Why did you bring your ball glove?" Penn asked.

Jim looked down at his glove as if it had grown there without his knowledge. He shrugged and slipped it off.

"Do you want to wear it?"

Penn bit his lower lip and considered.

"Maybe for a minute," he said.

Penn snapped the glove open and closed. He held it to his face and sniffed. He pounded the ball into the pocket. Jim stood and backed up a step and extended his hands. Penn tossed him the ball. Jim tossed it back to Penn. It bounced off of the heel of the glove onto the ground.

"I'll get it," Jim said.

"I just missed it," Penn said. "That's all."

They tossed the ball back and forth several times without speaking. Penn didn't miss it again.

"Everything works fine except this leg," he said.

He threw the ball back to Jim a little harder.

"You know that day down in Aliceville?" Jim asked.

Penn caught the ball and held it. He looked down at it and frowned.

"I don't want to talk about it," he said.

"Since Ty Cobb was on the Moon and all, I should have let you use the glove."

"It's all right," said Penn, without looking up. "It's your glove."

"No, I shouldn't have been so selfish," Jim said. "If I hadn't been so selfish, Ty Cobb could have seen both of us play ball."

"Stop it, Jim," Penn said.

"I'm just trying to apologize."

Penn leaned over and covered his face with the glove. He drew a deep breath, and his shoulders began to shake.

"Penn? What's the matter?"

"He saw me fall down!" Penn wailed into the glove. "Ty Cobb saw me fall down in the mud!"

Jim ran over and swatted Penn on the back.

"No, he didn't," he said. "Ty Cobb didn't see you fall down. I bet it wasn't even Ty Cobb. I bet it was just somebody who looked like Ty Cobb. And even if it was him, he probably wasn't looking out the window."

Penn knocked Jim's arm away.

"It was, too, him!" he said. "And you know it!"

Jim felt a sudden heat rise upward from his

neck, and out the top of his head. He felt himself wanting to cry. He scrunched his face up, but nothing happened. He rubbed his eyes with his fists, but his eyes remained dry.

"All I'm trying to say is that you're a better ballplayer than I am," Jim said. "I should've let you use the glove."

"I told you I didn't want to talk about it! How many times do I have to say that? Can't you hear? Are you dumb?"

Jim opened his mouth to tell Penn that he wasn't dumb, but remembered that Penn had polio. He looked toward the house, but the back door remained closed. He sat down in the chair beside Penn and rocked. He couldn't think of one person in the world he wasn't mad at.

After a while Penn sat up and leaned back, breathing heavily, his face splotched and red. He wiped his eyes with the back of his right hand.

"I'm sorry," he said.

"For what?" asked Jim.

"For crying like that."

"It's all right."

"No, it's not. I'm not a baby."

"I didn't say you were a baby."

"It's just that I'm tired. I never cry unless I'm really tired."

"I'm tired, too," said Jim. "We had a long trip." He yawned theatrically, closed his eyes, and leaned back in the chair.

"Let's just rest a minute," Penn said. "Then we can talk some more."

"Okay."

After a few minutes the fingers of Penn's throwing hand uncurled, and the ball dropped heavily onto the ground. Jim stood up and walked down to the creek. Its sandy bottom was dotted with periwinkles. He picked up a leaf and dropped it into the current. The shadow of the leaf slid over the periwinkles like the shadow of a cloud. As he turned away he saw a wheelchair parked behind a rhododendron on the creek bank. He started as if it were an animal. He hurried back to the rocking chairs and looked down at Penn.

Even though Penn's face was still red, he smiled slightly in his sleep. His breath whistled through his nose with a falling note. Jim reached down and touched his ball glove with a finger. He picked up the baseball and tossed it from hand to hand, measuring its comforting weight, before placing it in the pocket of the glove. He tiptoed away, looked back once, and broke into a run up the hill.

Uncle Zeno pulled the truck back onto the road. Jim slumped against the door.

"Are you sick, Doc?" he asked.

Jim kept his eyes closed.

"Just tired, is all."

"How was Penn?"

"He was fine."

"Where was everybody?"

"They're all in the backyard," Jim said. "I told everybody 'bye in the backyard."

"I see," said Uncle Zeno, glancing sideways at Jim. "Where's your ball glove? Did you forget your ball glove?"

Jim shook his head slowly.

"I gave it to Penn," he said.

A cord of muscle tightened briefly in Uncle Zeno's jaw. He took his foot off of the accelerator, but then sped up again.

"Oh," he said. "I see. Did Penn like it?"

"Yes, sir," said Jim. "He liked it a whole lot."

Jim didn't know which made him feel worse, giving his ball glove to Penn, or his impending introduction to his grandfather. In Jim's mind, Amos Glass had always shared a room with the other dark figures who haunted his mother's stories, ghosts and goblins and killers who roamed about looking for bad little boys to catch and take away—Pharaoh, Bloody Bones, Blackbeard. Mama had always sworn she would never let Amos Glass lay eyes on Jim, just as she had always said that, as long as he was good, nobody would come at night to steal him away. But now that he was on his way to Amos Glass's house, the door to that room suddenly seemed unlocked. For all Jim knew, the next time he went to bed, the awful face of Bloody Bones would appear outside his window, or a panther would say his name.

"What makes my granddaddy so mean?" he asked.

"Hmm," said Uncle Zeno. "That's hard to say. All of us have got meanness inside us, I guess, but most of us don't let it come out. Most of us can keep from saying the things we shouldn't say, and doing the things we shouldn't do."

"Do you have meanness inside you?"

"Some."

"Do you think I might turn out mean?"

Uncle Zeno made a fist and gently shook it at Jim.

"Not unless you want to get into a world of trouble."

Jim almost smiled. He pushed Uncle Zeno's arm away.

"I just don't want to turn out like my grand-daddy," he said.

"Do you know why your granddaddy got in so much trouble?"

"Because he was a moonshiner?"

"That's part of it," Uncle Zeno said. "Do you know why people get in trouble for making moon-shine?"

"Because it's a sin?"

"Besides that."

Jim shook his head.

"Because every time a man makes a gallon of liquor, he's supposed to pay a tax to the govern-ment."

"Oh."

"And if he doesn't pay the tax, the Revenue comes and busts up his still and puts him in jail. Now, in the old days, the Revenue didn't bother the folks up on the mountain much, and the folks on the mountain didn't bother the Revenue. It was just too good a way to get a bunch of people shot.

"What got your granddaddy in trouble was that he didn't know when to leave well enough alone. He made a special kind of moonshine called Cherry Bounce, and people liked it so much, they came from Charlotte and Spartanburg and Columbia and all over just to get a jar or two. And Amos was a hard worker, I'll give him that. If a wild cherry turned ripe on Lynn's Mountain, Amos Glass was there to pick it. He worked all the time, making liquor, and after a while he got rich. His downfall was that once he got rich, he wanted to get richer. So he built a big distillery up there on the mountain, right out in the open, across the road from his house. It was a long, brick building with copper stills that he had shipped down here all the way from up north somewhere.

"Naturally, the Revenue heard about what Amos was up to. Since they didn't have any choice but to go after him, they sent a couple of their best agents up here to hunt him down. But in a few days those boys came back empty-handed, scared half to death. Amos had caught them and tied them up and told them that the mountain was blockaded. He sent word to their boss that he would kill the next man the Revenue sent. And, if that wasn't bad enough, he mailed a letter to a newspaper in Charlotte announcing that Lynn's Mountain had seceded from the Union."

"Like in the War Between the States?"

"Just like that. Amos believed it was his God-given right to make Cherry Bounce. He said that's why God put cherry trees on *his* mountain in the first place. He didn't want the government telling him what to do, and he thought that everybody else hated the government as much as he did. He thought that if he started a ruckus, everybody else in these parts would rise up and fight like the Confederacy did in '61. Amos had been a captain under Jeb Stuart, and was still mad about the way things turned out the first time."

"What happened?"

"Well, what happened is that nobody except the Revenue paid him any attention. People liked his liquor, all right, but they didn't much care for him. They were afraid of Amos, but that's different from liking him. Besides, a lot of people up here had been for the North in the war. And a lot of people just thought he had gone crazy. So only a few old boys, fellows who made their living working for Amos anyway, mostly Gentines, joined his little army and loaded their squirrel rifles and waited for the Revenue to come."

"Did they come?"

"They came, all right. Amos kidnapping those agents and writing that letter to the newspaper had made the Revenue and the governor and everybody else mad enough to spit. They bowed up and sent seventy-five federal marshals and a Gatling gun up the mountain after him."

"Did they have a war?"

"Not much of one, Doc. Amos and his boys barricaded the road and waited on the Revenue, but when those Gentines saw just exactly how much Revenue had come, and got a look at that Gatling gun, they decided they didn't want to secede from the Union after all. Every one of them just disappeared into the woods. Old Amos saw what the score was and tried to hide, but he was old, and nobody would help him, and in just a day or two the Revenue caught him, hiding in a corncrib. They hauled him back to his house and burned his distillery down and made him watch. Your daddy said that watching that fire was the first thing he could remember. This was in 1904, and he was just a little fellow. That's probably why the Revenue didn't burn the house down, too. They didn't want to turn a woman and a little fellow out in the cold. They took Amos down the mountain and gave him life in prison, but let him out in nine years."

"And he was still mean when he got out?"

"Maybe even meaner. Amos didn't change a bit in Atlanta, except that he got older, and he lost his touch for making whiskey. They say that after he got back up here, he couldn't get a single batch of Cherry Bounce to turn out right. He either didn't cook it hot enough, or he cooked it too hot, and not a swallow of it turned out fit to drink. It would make you drunk, but it tasted terrible. They say that's why he was so bad to your daddy and your grandma. He had lost everything but his meanness."

"One time my daddy shot a hole in Amos Glass's still," Jim said.

"Your daddy was a brave man, Doc. People say Amos killed a man or two in his day, and for a lot less than what your daddy did to that still."

Jim though about his father crouched in the laurel, drawing a careful bead on Amos's still, and felt himself inflate with pride and bravery.

"My daddy wasn't scared of nothing," he announced.

"Are you afraid of Amos Glass?" asked Uncle Zeno.

"Nope," Jim lied.

"Good. 'Cause we're here."

Jim jerked up straight and looked around. They were driving through a cool wood of hemlock and laurel and tall white pine, but there was no sign of a house. Up ahead the road forded a riffling creek. Uncle Zeno stopped the truck in the middle of the ford. From downstream came the breathy roar of a waterfall. Upstream lay a wide, green pool that looked like a good place to swim and fish. On the far side of the pool, in the shallows near a bank of blooming laurel, a muddy cloud roiled the water.

"This is Painter Creek, Doc," Uncle Zeno said. "It comes out of three springs right up there. And it looks like something just crawled out of the water and slipped into that laurel."

"What do you think it was?" Jim asked.

"There ain't no telling," Uncle Zeno said, driving out of the creek onto the far bank.

Around the next curve lay a long, unpainted, shotgun house, whose gable end faced the road. Uncle Zeno stopped the truck before they pulled into the yard. The yard had grown up in broomsedge and stickweed, in which crouched a rusted-out Reo truck. The house looked deserted. It squatted beneath a sagging tin roof, high atop crumbling rock piers. Jim could see daylight beneath it from the yard on the far side. All down its flank, boards had sprung loose and curled back like shavings on a partially whittled stick. It was the longest, funniest-looking house Jim had ever seen. He might have laughed if he hadn't known who waited for him inside.

"That's your granddaddy's house," Uncle Zeno said.

"Yes, sir."

"He built it himself, right after the war."

"Why's it so long?"

"Well, everybody said Amos knew how to start building a house, he just didn't know how to stop."

"Oh."

"Amos just said it was one story high and five stories long."

"Is that where my daddy was born?"

"That's the place. He lived right there until he went down the mountain."

"Is my granddaddy in there now?"

"I imagine so. I've heard he's real sick. Are you ready?"

Before Jim could answer, two long-legged girls, fourteen or fifteen years old, sprang out of the laurel and bounded like deer toward the back of the house. Their hair was wet and tangled, and their dresses clung to their switching flanks as they ran.

"I saw them first," Uncle Coran called out from the back of the truck.

"Now we know what was swimming in the creek," said Uncle Zeno.

"Who are they?" asked Jim.

"I don't have any idea, but I expect we're going to find out."

Uncle Zeno pulled into the yard alongside the old Reo. Through the screen door, Jim could see all the way to the rear of the house, where the back door admitted a brilliant rectangle of light. In be-

tween the two doors, the house seemed ominously
dark. Uncle Zeno honked the horn, waited for a
few moments, then got out and started around the
truck. A girl's face poked out from behind the wall
to the right of the screen door, and just as quickly
disappeared. Another face, identical to the first,
poked out from the wall on the left, and likewise
vanished. Uncle Zeno stopped in his tracks.

"Hello, the house," he called out.

"Who are you?" demanded a girl's voice.

"Who are you?"

"We asked you first."

"I'm Zeno McBride, from Aliceville. Those are
my brothers, Coran and Al, in the back of the
truck. That's my nephew Jim Glass in the front
seat. He's Amos's grandson."

"Amos don't have no grandkids," said a second
voice.

"This is his boy Jim's boy," Uncle Zeno said.

No reply came from the house.

"It's the boy's birthday," Uncle Coran tried from
the back of the truck.

From inside the house Jim heard violent whis-
pering. The two faces appeared in the door again,
but after an instant disappeared behind their re-
spective walls.

"Amos ain't got no money," the first girl called
out.

"And if he's got anything hid, he owes it to our
daddy for us living here," said the second.

"You shouldn't have told them *that*," Jim heard
the first girl hiss.

Uncle Zeno took off his hat, smoothed his hair, and looked up as if considering prayer. Then he shoved his hat back onto his head.

"Now look here," he began sternly. "We didn't come up here looking for money. If money was lying around all over this yard, we wouldn't stoop to pick it up."

Inside the house everything was quiet. Finally, in unison, the girls slowly extended their heads. They were long-faced, but pretty, with brown eyes and pouty mouths. They looked more alike than Uncle Coran and Uncle Al. They bit their lower lips with their upper teeth while studying Jim and the uncles. Jim thought something about them looked a little wild. He didn't want to get out of the truck.

"If you don't want money, then what do you want?" asked the girl on the left.

"We just want Jim to meet Amos before it's too late," said Uncle Zeno. "Amos and Jim are the last of their kind. That's all."

The girls considered a minute, then turned and looked at each other. After a moment they turned their gaze back to the yard.

"You can see him, but you have to wait first," the girl on the right said.

"We're wet," said the girl on the left.

"Shut *up*," whispered the girl on the right.

"Well, we *are*."

"We'll wait out here," Uncle Zeno said. "Just let us know when you're ready."

The poison oak shrouding the distillery walls made them almost invisible against the surrounding un-

dergrowth. Jim couldn't see them until Uncle
Zeno outlined their shape in the air with a finger.

"That's all there is?" Jim asked.

"That's all that's left," said Uncle Zeno. "Amos
must hate to look at that."

Jim approached the ruin as if the poison oak
were capable of reaching out and entwining him.
A tapestry of vines rendered the door impassable,
but a Jim-sized gap remained between the vines
covering the hole where the window had been and
the window's low sill. He carefully stepped through
the gap, stood up, and found himself inside what
had once been a long, narrow room. A small forest
of ragged poplars had pushed up through the
floor; the floor was made of cement, but the cement was crumbling into earth. The trees grew
toward a blue rectangle of sky, though they had yet
to reach the height of the walls. The inside walls
were still free of poison oak, although runners
tipped with new leaves peered like scouts over the
tops of the walls, and sneaked in through the windows. The sun lit the leaves of the vines covering
the windows along the southern wall, and pro-
jected shadows tinted with green onto the floor.

Jim squeezed through the trees toward the far
wall, with no other goal in mind than reaching it.
He tried to imagine the floor without trees growing through it. He tried to imagine a roof separat-
ing the floor from the sky, his grandfather bent
over a bubbling still, the Revenue outside with
torches, but found that the pictures inside his head
held only shadows — vague, unlit forms whose
movements made no sense. The building simply

seemed too old to have ever been anything else. Not even saying *My daddy saw this building burn down* restored it enough for Jim to imagine anyone other than himself inside it.

When he reached the far wall, he slapped both hands against the brick as if reaching base in a difficult game. The floor around his feet was littered with lumps of charcoal, with broken pieces of glass and fragments of earthenware. Jim picked up a piece of cement and scratched "JIM" onto the wall. He threw the cement through the curtain of poison oak covering the nearest window. He squatted and filled his pockets with crockery shards, as if they were the things he had come all this way to find. Across the room, Uncle Zeno's face appeared in the gap between the vines.

"You better come on back, Doc," he said. "It's time."

The girls stood barefoot at the top of the steps, squeezed into little girls' Sunday dresses, their wet hair combed straight back and clutched by enormous bows.

"I'm Ada," said the girl on the left.

"I'm Beth," said the girl on the right.

"*Re*hobeth," said Ada.

Beth whirled angrily on her sister.

"It's in the Bible," she said.

"Hey," Ada said, regarding Uncle Coran and Uncle Al. "Are y'all twins?"

Uncle Coran and Uncle Al turned and looked at each other.

"No," said Uncle Coran.

A wisp of a smile passed across Ada's face. Her head slowly tipped to one side.

"How old are y'all?" she asked.

"How old do you think we are?" asked Uncle Coran.

"Not to change the subject," said Uncle Zeno, "but who's your daddy?"

Uncle Coran winked at Jim.

"Robley Gentine," said Beth.

"That makes Jim here your cousin. His grandma Amanda was Robley's sister."

"We know," Beth said regally. She didn't even look at Jim.

"How come y'all to live here?" asked Uncle Al.

"Because our daddy makes us," Ada said. "We hate it."

"No, we don't."

"Yes, we do. Amos is nasty. We want to live somewhere else."

Ada glared at Jim. He was afraid she was going to fly down off the porch.

"Can we see Amos?" asked Uncle Zeno.

"You can't come inside," said Ada.

"Our daddy said not to let anyone in the house," added Beth.

"You can look in there," Ada said, pointing at the window to the right of the front door. "He's laying in the bed."

Jim left the uncles and mounted the steps. Ada and Beth moved aside, and he stepped past them onto the porch. His feet did not seem attached to his body. He watched his brogans moving across the weathered boards, and felt as if he were flying above them, watching them from a great height. He reached out and gingerly touched the screen covering the window with his fingertips. When he leaned closer to the screen, a sour stink rushed out and tried to push him back; he could taste the stench and the rusty wire in the back of his throat.

As his eyes adjusted to the light, he made out a bed pushed close to the window. In the center of the bed lay an old man, naked except for a sheet bunched around his waist. His body appeared to be constructed of sharp sticks, covered with the gray paper of a hornets' nest. Yellowed claws twisted from the ends of his fingers and toes. His head lay in a matted nest of long white hair; a bramble of scraggly white beard sprouted on his sunken cheeks. From the dark oval of his mouth came a liquid, metallic rasping. Jim realized in a helpless rush that his grandfather was going to die soon.

While Jim's mother and uncles had known and lived with Jim Glass, Sr., and Jim had constructed a man named Daddy from their stories, nothing had made Jim's father so real as the beating heart of Amos Glass. He had always felt as if he were playing a type of game with his father, that his father was just out of sight ahead of him, watching as Jim looked behind this door, or under that bed. And, although he knew that such things didn't happen, he had always secretly felt as if tomorrow might be the day he tracked his daddy down, that tomorrow he might meet him on a path in the woods, or find him sitting on a rock by the river. But now he understood that Amos made this possible. Once Amos died, Jim's father would become as ancient and faceless as a man in the Bible, a man walking away until he is finally impossible to see. Once Amos was gone, Jim would be alone in the world in a way he had never been alone before.

Jim leaned forward until his nose brushed the screen. Amos breathed with the startled desperation of a fish washed up onto a creek bank, searching the harsh light and unfamiliar air for the things he needed but had left behind in the world he knew. Jim saw his young father step out into a road, his belongings stuffed into a sack. He looked toward Jim and waved. Jim softly scraped the screen with a fingernail. He felt weak, as if he didn't have the strength to push his voice through the wire.

"Granddaddy?" he whispered.

His father turned and started down the road.

"Granddaddy? It's me. Jim."

His legs almost gave way when Amos opened his eyes. Amos's eyes were the brilliant, fierce blue about which Jim had heard in stories, except now the color was filtered through milky cataracts, like the sky reflected in water, or seen through opaque glass.

"Hey, Granddaddy," Jim said. "I came to see you."

When Amos didn't answer, Jim tilted his head slightly in order to align his face with the old man's stare. But no matter where he moved, his grandfather's gaze always seemed focused someplace else, in some far distance Jim could not occupy. When his grandfather's eyes closed again, Jim lifted his fingertips away from the screen and turned to Ada and Beth.

"He doesn't know who I am," Jim said.

"He don't know nobody, no more," said Ada.

Jim climbed onto a small boulder that jutted out of the mountainside at the bald near the head of the valley. He was almost as tall as the uncles. At their feet the mountain fell away into air. The late-afternoon sunlight seemed to rise from someplace below them.

"How do you like the view from up here, Doc?" Uncle Zeno asked.

Jim shrugged. He didn't know where to look, nor what to say. The green countryside did not contain a shape or a landmark that he recognized. He had spent his whole life in a single place, looking up at a mountain; he had never considered how different that place might look from the mountain's top. The world he had known all his life did not seem related to the world he saw now.

"Which way is home?" he asked.

Uncle Zeno pointed at the valley beneath them.

"See, there in the middle? That's the road we drove in on."

Jim picked out the road, the red dirt faintly glowing in the sun. Near the road, a small herd of cows pulled their shadows through a pasture.

"Now, look on the other side of the road," Uncle Coran said. "Do you see that strip of brush? That's Painter Creek."

Jim saw water, glittering with sunlight, through an open spot in the trees. He nodded.

"Now follow the creek toward the river and you'll find home," said Uncle Al.

The creek twisted into the hills they had driven through that morning, and wandered out the other side. Jim traced its course until he was sure of its direction, then allowed his vision to fly ahead until it cut the state highway stretched tight across the countryside. On the far side of the highway lay the railroad. He followed the highway and the railroad east until he saw the corrugated sides of the uncles' cotton gin glinting in the sun.

Once he located the cotton gin, Jim easily found the store and the depot and the uncles' houses; he found the school and the spot of red dirt where the town boys and the mountain boys had played baseball. He cataloged the church and the hotel, the houses, barns, and sheds, until he was sure that everything was in its place. He could not believe how little space Aliceville occupied in the world. He realized that if it had disappeared during his absence, the world would not have noticeably changed. In his mind's eye he tried to draw the circle around Aliceville that his great-grandfather McBride had surveyed, but found that it didn't make him feel better. He realized that there was nothing he could do inside that circle that would matter much to anyone outside it.

As the sun began to set, Jim and the uncles watched the last yellow light of the day slide up the

mountain toward the bald, dragging evening behind it. When the light went out of their faces, they
turned and watched it retreat up the peak, where
at the summit a single tree flared defiantly before
going dark. A chilly breeze whipped from nowhere
across the bald and flapped the legs of Jim's overalls. He turned with the uncles for a last look at the
view before heading down the mountain. All but
the brightest greens had drained out of the world,
leaving in their stead an array of somber blues. A
low fog had begun to seep out between the trees
along Painter Creek. Jim jumped down from the
rock and looked again toward home. A single light
blinked on at Uncle Zeno's.

"Cissy," Uncle Coran said. "She turned on the
porch light."

"We shouldn't have left her by herself all this
time," said Uncle Al. "One of us should've stayed
home."

Through the distance the light seemed to
flicker, as if struggling to remain lit against the
great emptiness around it. Jim closed his eyes.
Mama stood on the porch, staring up at the mountain, wondering where he was. She sat down in the
snow in front of the tenant house. Penn's fingers
uncurled and the baseball dropped into the grass.
His grandfather stared past him with milky blue
eyes. Ada and Rehobeth followed Uncle Coran
and Uncle Al to the truck, chewing on their lower
lips. Whitey gave him a baseball; he threw it and hit
Penn in the back. Abraham handed him a piece of
apple. His father walked toward him across a cot-

ton field; he dropped his hoe, took another step, and fell onto the ground.

When Jim opened his eyes, he saw Uncle Zeno's face swimming inches from his own. Uncle Al and Uncle Coran knelt on either side of him.

"Hey, hey, shh," Uncle Zeno said. "What's the matter?"

Jim waved an arm out at the world beyond the end of the mountain.

Uncle Zeno frowned and shook his head.

"It's too big," Jim said.

"What is?"

"Everything."

"I don't understand, Doc."

"I'm just a boy," he said.

Uncle Zeno rocked back on his heels. He looked at Uncle Coran and Uncle Al, then smiled at Jim.

"We know that," he said. "But you're *our* boy."